PRAISE FOR EARL JAVORSKY'S FIRST
CHARLIE MINER NOVEL, DOWN SOLO:

"Earl Javorsky's bold and unusual *Down Solo* blends the mysterious and the supernatural boldly and successfully. The novel is strong and haunting, a wonderful debut."
- T. Jefferson Parker, *New York Times* bestselling author of *Full Measure* and *The Famous and the Dead*

"Awesome"
- James Frey, *New York Times* bestselling author

"Don't miss Earl Javorsky's *Down Solo*. It's kick-ass, man. Excellent writing. This guy is the real deal."
- Dan Fante, author of the memoir *Fante* and the novel *Point Doom*

"Javorksy's writing reminded me of the Carl Hiaasen novels I'd read sprawled out on the deck on one sunny Florida vacation. Perfect entertainment, with the right amount of action to keep me alert (and to keep me from snoozing myself into a sunburned state). But there's also a deeper layer in *Down Solo*, which left me thinking past the final page."
- Bibliosmiles

"Javorsky's dark and gritty prose is leavened with just enough humor to make *Down Solo* a compelling story that will take readers to the outer limits of noir."
- *San Diego City Beat*

Down to No Good

DOWN TO NO GOOD
EARL JAVORSKY

This is a work of fiction. Names, characters, places, and incidents either are the product of the author's imagination or are used fictitiously. Any resemblance to actual events, locales, organizations, or persons living or dead is entirely coincidental and beyond the intent of either the author or the publisher.

The Story Plant
Studio Digital CT, LLC
P.O. Box 4331
Stamford, CT 06907

Print ISBN-13: 978-1-61188-253-7
E-book ISBN: 978-1-945839-10-8

Visit our website at www.TheStoryPlant.com

First Story Plant paperback printing: October 2017

0 9 8 7 6 5 4 3 2 1

To those on the firing line,
working toward an alternative
to the so-called War on Drugs
and helping where they can.

As I approach the state of pure euphoria
my eyes are gringo spies and I
may anytime be changed to birds
by a Tungus explosion that controls time
but I am no apocalyptic kid
and cannot sleep because of the thunder
under the summer afternoon
and my dumb bird's eye starts
out of my head
and flies around the world

Lawrence Ferlinghetti, *Euphoria*

Chapter 1

I wake up looking down at my body, naked on a gurney at the morgue.

No.

That's a memory.

This has happened to me before.

I was riding my bike, working a case, high as a meteorite that doesn't yet know it's about to crash and burn, still happily tooling along in space, at night, wrapped in a warm blanket of summer air, Jack Daniels, and a smidgen of heroin. Some creep shot me in the temple, and I woke up hovering above my own corpse.

This time is different.

Not a gurney. Not the morgue.

A bed. My body, eyes closed, on a bed. I've got a bird's-eye view, hovering like a kite, still tethered, but barely, by an invisible string.

Let's get clear on my condition. I don't know what it is, but I know what it is not. I am not a vampire, or a zombie, or a ghost. I'm not a thousand years old, I have no superpowers, and I've never been a hero. What I do have is a broken life, a broken family, and, so far, an inexplicable inoculation against dying. And a daughter I would die for—or, in this case, return to life for.

The tether reels me in. I descend toward the body, a mirror image to it, my arms at my sides, my feet slightly apart. Three bullet holes in my face—and one in my gut—are going to need some repair. At contact, I am absorbed and no longer looking down at myself but looking up at the ceiling.

I stretch my fingers, curl them into fists, and stretch them again.

"Jesus holy fucking Christ!"

I know that voice.

I turn my head. It's awkward, after the lightness of floating, to be in the body, to know its heaviness and vulnerability. There's a man sitting in a chair next to the bed. He's a cop, and the first thing I think is: *He knows my secret. Now he really knows it.* But it's okay, because he's also my friend and I trust him. I have to.

"Hey, Dave, how's it going?" My voice sounds artificial—a forced process of pushing air, modulating vibrations with my vocal cords, shaping syllables with my mouth and tongue. I make my lips grin.

Dave sits there like a stuffed panda in his rumpled white shirt and cheap black sports coat. There's blood on his clothes. It's in his fingernails—my blood, dried and caked on his hands. His right hand is clasped around a Heineken, which he finally tilts to his mouth and drains.

I force the body up and into a sitting position, feet on the floor. I flex my fingers a few more times, roll my shoulders, and look at Dave. For a moment, I close my eyes and leave the body, just as an experiment, and roam around the room. From over Dave's shoulder I watch it slump back into the pillows like a marionette whose strings have been cut. Dave stands and moves toward the bed, but I slip back into the body and work my mouth and tell him it's okay.

I sit back up and ask Dave, "Why am I naked?"

"Because you were shot full of holes and clinically dead. I brought you back to my place and cleaned you up. I took off your clothes to see how many more bullets there might be in you. Your things are right over there." He points to a chair in the corner.

"You're taking this pretty well."

He shrugs. "I feel like I'm in a bad movie, but hey . . ."

"I appreciate your bringing me here."

"I knew if I called the paramedics you'd have been sliced and diced at the coroner's."

"How long have I been here?"

Dave looks at his watch. "It's noon. Call it thirty-six hours."

"What day is it? And date?"

"Wednesday. Last day in August."

I stand and walk to the chair to get dressed. Roaming—moving freely out of the body—is easier than this, but I'll adjust. I have before. The gorilla-suit quality of living in the body becomes commonplace, the intentional management of operating the system, beating the heart, making the blood run in the veins, the conscious act of breathing: all of it becomes second nature.

It's almost like being alive.

CHAPTER 2

Wednesday, August 31

Dave Putnam had been a cop for over thirty years, but nothing had prepared him for the last thirty-six hours.

The whole fiasco had started with Charlie Miner, whom he had known and even occasionally worked with over the years, calling him and asking for a favor. Offering him a deal. Twisting his arm a bit with a preposterous story, telling him he'd prove it and that Dave could take several murders off the books. Celebrities. Big money. An investment scam.

And, against his better judgment, Dave had gone along. Two days ago, he had transported Charlie's daughter over the border from Tijuana—the favor—and that night met Charlie at a restaurant to hear him pitch his case. Later, when he got Charlie's text, he went to the agreed-upon location to back Charlie's play and round up the perpetrators.

In the meantime, he'd had a few too many. It made him sloppy, and it made him late. So, instead of calling for backup and showing up fresh and ready, he played cowboy. He took his biggest gun, an unregistered Desert Eagle .50 caliber that his father had given him, out of his trunk and left the restaurant parking lot with the gun on the passenger seat, squinting out at the road and concentrating on staying in his lane.

He got lost in Santa Monica Canyon and had to backtrack to the Coast Highway and try again. This time he wound up on Amalfi Drive, heading up toward Pacific Palisades. The frustration called for a hit off the pint he kept under the seat.

When he finally got to the site, he came around the side of the house and saw a man with a silenced gun standing over two bodies. One of them was Charlie Miner's. When he saw the silencer swing up to point at him, Dave fired. The bullet blew the man into a hole that had clearly just been dug in the yard. The noise was ridiculous, but it clarified the situation: Dave hoisted Charlie's body over his shoulder and started back toward his car. As an afterthought, he went back and picked up one of several SentrySafe H2300 cases nestled in the dirt.

^

Now he was sitting in his apartment, watching Charlie Miner's corpse, studying it as if for a clue, an answer, perhaps, to the mystery of why he, Dave, had behaved so badly. Leaving the scene of an officer-involved shooting. Stealing from a crime scene. Hiding a body.

The first two he could justify: he was tanked, and the case he took out of the ground just looked interesting.

But taking Charlie Miner's body, with three bloody holes in its face, and dumping it in the back seat of his car, and then driving home and carrying it to his apartment—there was no explaining that.

Except . . .

Dave had known there was something off about Charlie. Not just off, but weird. More than weird—inexplicable. Dave had dug up morgue photos of an unidentified DOA, gunshot wounds, that had somehow disappeared. And though he had denied it, Charlie Miner was the guy in the photos.

And so the vigil. Turn the phone ringer off. Stick to beer. Wash the blood off Charlie's face. Watch the body. Nod off now and then.

Watch the body.

It happened at noon. He was about to doze when he saw a finger twitch. Then the fingers on both hands flexed, curled into fists, and flexed again.

Chapter 4

Time passes in a dream. My phone tells me it's the thirty-first of October. In the two months since I was resurrected in Dave's apartment, the weather has gone from sunny and hot to an unusual California chill, and my mind has gone in and out of functioning mode. Sometimes I sit and stare at a wall and see nothing but a gray fog. Lifting a hand to my face to scratch an itch or bat away an insect takes too much effort. Other times I see into the wall, into the atoms and the blur of their electron shells and the enormous space within; I see galaxies receding, and I sense the end of time approaching. And, with gradually increasing frequency, I'm back in the world, brushing my teeth, making omelets for my daughter Mindy and myself, trying to pick up the pieces of my life.

The pieces of my life:

I own a blackened patch of land where my house used to be in Mar Vista, just off Venice Boulevard.

I have a teenage daughter and an ex-wife who will kill each other if I don't keep them apart. Allison was the love of my life until I squandered it all for opiates. What's left is a toxic stew of divorce, recriminations, and custody battles. Thank God I've still got Mindy.

I have a friend Jimmy, who used to be my heroin dealer and is now recovering from his own bullet wounds, although in the traditional manner, under a doctor's care.

I am the proud owner of two million dollars' worth of gold bars, although selling them will be tricky and laundering the cash even trickier. Jimmy's working on it.

Then there's the matter of Daniel, who visited me the other day.

The memories arise, like bubbles from the depths of a swamp, then disappear or merge with other memories and make a new kind of sense, or no sense, and I have trouble with time: good times, bad times, future times, past times—

Yesterday: blank.

Two months ago:

^

Wednesday, August 31

Dave Putnam is a hell of a writer. He's a cop, but he's a scribbler at heart. He types like Herbie Hancock plays the piano. Voices emerge, characters, madness; epic stories get banged out on his worn laptop. Dave's seen it all. He's got tales to tell.

He stares at me as I come out of his bathroom, eyes popping as he registers my newly repaired face.

"I don't know if I could even make sense of this in a story," he says.

"Who would read it?"

"Beats me. Maybe there's some hybrid reader geek out there—like a mix between a Stephen King fan and an Elmore Leonard fan."

"You think it'd be hard to write?"

He shrugs.

I tell him, "Try living it." And, of course, there's that word: Living.

Dave's place is in Culver City. My fifteen-year-old daughter, Mindy, has been holed up in an apartment in Venice. The creep who shot me the first time lived there with his halfwit brute of a roommate until we had an encounter in a cave in the mountains near Ensenada. They're still in the cave.

^

We leave Dave's. The blazing sun and the desert winds put a hot crackle in the air. My phone is full of desperate texts and voicemail from Mindy. Dave is driving, heading west on Washington Boulevard. I hit Mindy's number on speed dial.

"Dad! Tell me it's you."

"Yes. Where are you? We're coming to get you."

"I'm home. I mean the apartment. Where have you been? Who's 'we'? Oh my God, Dad . . ." She's sobbing, and I'm staring out the window at the shabby storefronts and the world is golden because I have Mindy to come home to.

When she was young, and I still had a family, we would make up stories together at bedtime. A mythical creature called a greyborg would transport her through the tunnel of sleep to the land of dreams, where she could fly, solve mysteries, and slay dragons. Years later, even in my darkest times, we would joke about the greyborg.

Now she's almost sixteen, a walking canvas of fantastical images, with crazy hair and a lopsided smile and a fundamental goodness that makes me grateful every time I see her.

Dave and I pull up to the Flora, a run-down, two-story stucco box on a tired little street in the

Oakwood section of Venice, where gentrification hasn't yet pushed out the poor and the barely-hanging-on working class. The broken gate scrapes concrete as I push it open, triggering a ferocious snarling and clattering of nails against the door of the left front unit and explosive staccato barking from the right.

Dave yells at me from his car. "You gonna be all right?"

I shrug.

I don't even know what that means. But Mindy'll be there, so there's hope.

Chapter 5

Dave watched Charlie Miner go up the dilapidated stairs of the crummy building, wondering how much of his worldview would have to change to accommodate what he had seen over the past few days. Although, earlier events—involving a series of cases—had already put a large crack in his certainty about life being rational.

As he drove toward work, his mind shifted to the crime scene in Santa Monica Canyon.

The good news was that he had managed to get to his car and out of the neighborhood unnoticed. The bad news was that there was a .50 caliber bullet in a dead body, and no gun to match. Okay, so he'd have to ditch the gun. He could get an easy grand for it, but then it could bounce back on him if some idiot got caught with it and rolled over. And, given what he'd found when he broke open the SentrySafe case he had found, sacrificing the Desert Eagle was the way to go. Besides, he still had his standard issue 9 mm and a backup.

The case had been surprisingly heavy when he pulled it out of the ground. There were several of them in the hole. He was already carrying Charlie's body and almost said *fuck it*, but grabbed it on a hunch. Three people were dead, and Dave wanted to know why. Sometime during his vigil over Charlie's body, he had jimmied the lock on the case and pried open the lid. Nestled in black foam like expensive camera equipment were two bricks, each with a stamp that said 999.9 *Fine Gold*.

So, dump the gun. Lie low on the gold. Do some footwork on how to get cash for it without drawing any attention. Meanwhile, it was time to let Charlie Miner put his life—or whatever it was—back together. Dave was still a cop, and it was time to see what the job had in store for him.

CHAPTER 6

We settled into the apartment. Mindy kept house while I healed and remembered and forgot and dreamed. Sometimes it's hard to tell the difference, and I'll have a sudden flash of memory only to jettison it as a dream fragment.

Over time, in several sittings, sometimes lucid and other times probably raving, I filled Mindy in on the truth about my condition. When I raved, she probed, gently.

"What do you mean, *dead*?"

"I was in the morgue, on a gurney."

"Ah, Dad, maybe the hospital? And you walked out before they could help you?"

"No, it was the morgue. I was naked and had to take clothes off another body. And that was just the first time."

She never called me crazy. Her eyes would well up, she'd put her hand on mine, and sometimes we would just sit in silence.

At one point, I told her about Daniel and how he had appeared at the morgue and driven me home and later became my mentor.

"What do you mean, *mentor*?" she asked.

"He helps me navigate my new reality. He understands it."

"How?"

"I have no idea." In her young wisdom, she allowed me what she was sure were my fantasies and soothed me when I became agitated.

^

Monday, October 3l, night

It must be Halloween today; kids in costumes from Walmart and Target are being shepherded along the street below by sketched-out parents watching over their shoulders for trouble. Like me. There's trouble coming, but I can't remember where it's coming from. Or why.

Sometime during this past week—I think it was Wednesday—I had a visit from Daniel.

^

Originally, Daniel was my facilitator at a treatment program for heroin addicts. He once drove me across the border to their clinic in Mexico, where they gave me a hallucinogenic drug cocktail and performed a sort of shamanistic exorcism that resulted in my first experience of separating from my body. Apparently, I was one of their losers, as I repressed the whole experience and went home and kept getting loaded.

The next time I saw Daniel, he picked me up from the morgue in LA, where—dead with a bullet in my temple—I had mysteriously awakened on a gurney, and drove me to my home. And then he just kept appearing in my life. At one point he told me that I was his responsibility, and that fulfilling it was the key to the perpetuation of his own revival from an otherwise permanent overdose.

On this particular occasion, he showed up at our door and called my name without knocking. I don't know how he found me, but he always seems to know where I am. I opened the door and waved him in. Where he had previously had dreadlocks and a Caribbean accent, he now wore a well-tailored suit and had close-cropped hair flecked with gray, his skin even darker than the chocolate shade of his tie. At the curb downstairs was an expensive new Lexus.

I introduced Daniel to Mindy, who asked if she could get him anything. He declined; his accent, if anything, was slightly upper-crust Boston. He had once explained to me that his work required him to assimilate in various environments, but he never told me where he was originally from.

Daniel looked around the cramped, shabby living room. Mindy had tidied and cleaned, but the decor still spoke to the fact that we were campers here: there were T.S.O.L posters on the wall, miniature Harley choppers on the kitchen counter, and a dangling dried blowfish lamp that spun lazily over the sofa.

"You look well, Charlie Miner," he said, nodding slightly in approval. "Like a hermit crab, taking over an abandoned home."

I hadn't thought of it that way and felt defensive. "You seem to know everything about me, so you must know that the previous tenant torched my house. This just worked out as a convenient backup for us."

Daniel said, "Yes, and he and his friend are conveniently absent. But that's not why I'm here."

I was developing a nice resentment. Jason Hamel Junior, whom I had nicknamed Ratboy because of his unfortunate features and furtive, malicious manner, had not only burned down my house, he had kidnapped my daughter and tried to kill me. I wasn't interested in reviewing the details of his death.

Daniel took a seat under the blowfish. I settled into a ratty orange beanbag cushion while Mindy sat on a barstool and examined the Harleys. I could tell, though, that she was paying close attention to our visitor.

"I'm here to remind you of an obligation," Daniel said. He could have been a banker calling in a loan, or a prosecutor about to read an indictment, but he was talking about a different currency and set of laws altogether.

The cushion put me almost on the floor and in an awkward position for the level of discourse Daniel was heading toward. I said, "Look, I'm glad to be alive. Now I intend to go about the business of living life." It sounded lame as it came out.

"Your second chance—make that *third chance*—at life is a gift, but it's not entirely free."

I noticed Mindy looking up, her eyes narrowed—they flicked my way in surprise and then back to the Harleys.

My Mexican detox ritual involved the hallucinogen ibogaine. The treatment center was called Second Chance at Life, although the second chance they offered was of the more mundane variety: freedom from opiate addiction. Reviving people post mortem was not in their purview, but my experience during the ceremony had in some inexplicable way set the stage for all that was to follow, and Daniel had made it his personal mission to guide me through each transition.

I said, "It's a gift, or there's a cost; make up your mind," feeling petulant and wanting him to go.

Daniel shook his head slightly, his smile one a schoolteacher might give to a slow student. "It's in the posture of receiving that you can keep it or lose it. Imagine a man dying of thirst in the desert. He comes upon a woman with a pail of water, and she pours some out for him. Only by cupping his hands can he drink."

We were beating around a burning bush here, and I wanted him to get to the point so I could say no, and thanks for everything but it's time for you to go help someone else now. "What is it you want me to do?"

"The same thing I do. Be prepared to show up when someone's on the threshold and about to cross over. Guide them back, if they're meant to return."

"How do I know that?"

"You'll know."

"When am I supposed to do this?"

"Right now. Just be willing."

I showed him to the door. I had better things to do.

^

Mindy said, "So that's Daniel."

"If I'm crazy, he's in on it too."

She looked at me for a long time. I waited. Finally, she said, "He seems to have ideas about what you should do."

"He does indeed."

"Maybe you should listen to him."

CHAPTER 7

Thursday, October 27

The day after Daniel's visit, I got a call from Dave. It was not a good day for me; I was teetering between mental acuity and total vacuity. He asked me how I was doing and I drew a blank. I got hung up on the "how" part and took a detour into *How am I even here at all? How do I formulate thoughts? How does a thought become words?* After a long silence, he said, "I may need your help on something."

My first reaction was one of irritation. Another person was trying to get me to engage in a bigger world than I was interested in. The fog of my fugue state had been lifting incrementally, and my capacity to help anyone was questionable.

But this was Dave, who had carried my dead body from a crime scene and parked it at his apartment until I could find my way back to it.

The thought that finally turned into words was, "Why me?"

^

I agreed to meet for coffee. It was time to road test my new self, to get out and drive and be around other people and see if I could pull it off. I told Mindy I was off to do an errand, and that we were going to have to figure something out about where to live and how to enroll her in school. All she said

30

was, "I'm not going back to Mom's." I couldn't argue with that. The last time we had seen Allison she had been in fine form, boiled as an owl at nine in the morning, wearing a tattered bathrobe and high heels and screaming at us as she threw Mindy's packed suitcase at my car.

I found Dave waiting for me at The Pygmy Up, my favorite coffee dive and the closest thing I have to an office now that my house is a charred brick chimney surrounded by a pile of ashes. He was settled into an overstuffed armchair with his feet up on a mismatched ottoman, holding a frothy dessert coffee and a scone. There was a faux-leather folio on the little table next to him, along with an iPad and a book with a picture of a smiling blond woman on the cover. The place was packed, and I had to sit on a footstool, which made me feel like the shortest guy in the room.

"You watch the news?" It seemed Dave had learned his lesson about engaging me in small talk.

"Some," I said. Soaps, Netflix, the news: all were threaded into the strange dream of my recent experience, and separating fact from fiction—always a tough job—eluded me entirely. "I heard something about some crazies taking over a government building in Oregon."

"Yeah, well, it pays to be white if you're gonna pull a stunt like that. This is about a case I've got going, and a few before it that all tie together."

"Why in the world do you think I can help?" I had spent the last ten years working as a private investigator, but until the case that got me shot, got my daughter kidnapped, took me to Mexico, and got me shot again, my work was pretty mundane: insurance fraud, cheating wives, and missing persons kept the rent paid and food on the table.

Dave sipped at his coffee and wiped the foam from his lip. Then he put the drink down and said, "First of all, you're a sharp guy, and we've worked together in the past. But the real reason is that there's some shit going on that's outside my range of experience and more in line with yours. And . . ." He trailed off and just stared at me, then shrugged and shook his head slightly. "Fuck it. Maybe it's a bad idea."

I took the bait. "What do you mean, more in line with mine?"

The place jangled with people talking, chairs scraping, and Lester Young playing in the background—the owner is an old jazz musician who used to play bass with Yusef Lateef. It's about forty steps away from the nearest weed dispensary, so it's full of hipsters with goofy-looking beards, Venice bodybuilders, dreadlocked surfers, and even a few old-school beat characters. Dave chomped a bite of his scone and brushed the crumbs off his lap.

"Well, you've got this"—he gestured, a sort of flip of his hand into the air—"Jesus, I don't even know what to call it. Your condition. Whatever it is, it's weird. It's outside of the ordinary shit that I deal with, and so is this case I'm talking about."

"So you've got some fringe thing going on, and you think I'm an expert on all things fringe because of my condition?"

"I don't know about expert. I just think that you have a broader range of experience that might put this in context." The Pygmy Up's resident cat ambled over, brushed against my legs, and then jumped up on Dave's lap, taking a swipe at his scone. Dave backhanded it to the floor and eyed the pastry dubiously.

"Okay, what is it?"

Dave reached for the folio and extracted a handful of news clippings and handed me the top two. "Here, see for yourself."

The first one was dated December 8 of last year.

Billy Taft's Body Found
with Help from Psychic

The body of fifteen-year-old Billy Taft, who had been missing since November 5, was found by Los Angeles police after a month-long investigation. The search had frustrated authorities until Tamara Gale, a local woman who claims to be a psychic, offered her assistance.

According to Detective Dave Putnam, Ms. Gale contacted him in early December, claiming to have information that could lead to the missing teen's whereabouts. Her offer was initially dismissed when it became apparent that she claimed knowledge through what she called "heightened faculties of awareness."

"We tend to be skeptical regarding information that comes from unconventional sources," said Putnam. "However, when Ms. Gale persisted and furnished us with a credible lead, we had to set aside our bias."

Police have not released details of Ms. Gale's contribution to the investigation, but do credit her with (continued on back page)

I looked over at Dave and all I could come up with was, "Really? What did she tell you? This isn't very specific."

"Yeah, well, we didn't give up the specifics. She said she had a vision of a boy wearing a blue jacket, lost in the desert. Then she said she saw a hungry dog, and the boy couldn't move."

"So how did that help you find him?"

"She said the desert had airplanes. Then she said they weren't airplanes, just propellers—a lot of them, and that there was a thing like a ski lift, and if you went on it you could see a boulder in a canyon."

I could picture the San Gorgonio Pass Wind Park, which is a huge wind-generator farm, and the Palm Springs Aerial Tramway, which has a gondola that goes from Coachella Valley almost to the top of San Jacinto Peak.

"That would be Chino Canyon. Lots of boulders there."

"We went out with Riverside County sheriffs and their dogs. Found the body—what was left of it—hidden by an overhanging boulder formation. Coyotes had gotten to it."

"Did anything lead to a suspect?"

Dave shook his head. "Not this time, but read the next one."

This time the date was April 14, just over six months ago.

Psychic Who Helped Police Scores Again

The case of a missing teen has been solved with the help of Tamara Gale, the famed psychic who gained national attention for her assistance last year in the solving of Billy Taft's abduction and murder.

Seventeen-year-old Kyle Johnson's body was found in a drainpipe at a Santa Monica beach. Johnson, a Brentwood resident, had been missing for ten days, but police were reluctant to mount a full-scale investigation. According to Detective Dave Putnam, "The victim had a record of drug offenses and had run away from home on numerous occasions over the previous four years. We had no reason to allocate resources beyond issuing a missing-person report."

Johnson's absence did make the local news, however, as his father, Elliot Johnson, is one of Hollywood's most successful directors. Mr. Johnson made a direct plea to the public, saying that his son had been drug-free and enthusiastic about graduating high school.

The coroner's office released a statement that Kyle Johnson died of blunt-force trauma to the side of the head. Evidence found on the body has led to the arrest of a local man. Johnson's father has publicly thanked Ms. Gale for her help in the case. Her response was that he should thank her "spirit guide, who has been with me since (continued on Page 4)

I had never thought much of psychics, faith healers, UFO conspiracies, and crystal-ball gazing, but that was before I had had first-hand experience with the unexplainable. Still, I found myself skeptical. I handed the copies back and said, "What do you think?"

Dave shrugged. "I don't know what to think. Sounds like horseshit to me, and we tried to blow her off, but then she came back with good information."

"How do you think she got it?"

"She says her spirit guide told her. What the fuck am I supposed to do with that?"

"Is there any way that she could be connected to the perpetrators?" This seemed like the only possible conclusion.

"We looked into her pretty deep. She's got no record, no known association with either victim or the guy that killed the Johnson kid, and no reason to come to us with a bogus story about hearing voices from the other side. She even has a book out on her life and how she discovered her so-called special gift. Here, I brought you a copy." He handed me the book, a hardcover titled *Yesterday, Today, and Tamara: My Life as a Psychic*. The author, Tamara Gale, looked like an over-the-hill beauty queen, some thirty years and thirty pounds past her prime but still photogenic and projecting the charm and confidence of someone used to getting what she wants.

The back cover told me this about the author: *Psychic to the Stars! Speaker for the Departed! Consultant to the LAPD!* I asked Dave, "What stars?" and he shrugged. "Did your people okay this 'consultant' bit?"

"She didn't ask."

I flipped it open to a random page toward the beginning and read out loud:

> I met my first husband at a party. He was the tall, dark stranger across the room, and my heart melted the second we locked eyes. I knew he was my soul mate as he glided toward me through

the chattering crowd, which seemed to part as if knowing that something foreordained was about to take place.

I thumbed to the end and noted the page number. "So you want me to read two hundred and eighty-six pages of this?"

This time Dave handed me an iPad, which he had already turned on and cued to a YouTube video. The picture frozen on the screen showed Tamara Gale and what appeared to be a talk-show host sitting in chairs and facing the camera but angled toward each other. Tamara Gale had her eyes closed, her head tilted back as if she were trying to remember something; the host was leaning forward, apparently listening intently. I tapped the "play" arrow.

Tamara's voice blared out of the device's small speaker, competing with the noise of the coffee shop, but I could still make out what she was saying:

> I see a bird . . . it flies like a hummingbird, and it swoops down and then hovers over . . . (long pause as she moves her hand in a vaguely circular motion above her head) . . . I see young people, with books—No! They're at a sports event, and they're bending over. Now they're rolling on the ground—

She stopped abruptly and opened her eyes, looking straight into the camera, and then broke into tears. She went on: "Something terrible is going to happen, I don't know when or where. Oh my God, we have to do something!"

Dave motioned for me to hand him back the device. He turned it off and set it back on the table and then handed me another news clipping, saying, "This is from yesterday, five days after she was on that show. It first ran in some small-town newspaper in New Mexico, on the edge of the Navajo Nation, but then it hit the national news."

Ricin Poisoning at New Mexico High School Football Game

AP—Eleven students at Tohatchi High School in Tohatchi, New Mexico, are being treated for acute ricin poisoning that was apparently delivered by a miniature drone during a football game. According to one of the victims, "It buzzed around like a hummingbird. We thought it was cool, like maybe it was taking pictures of us, and then it swooped down and sprayed something like a tiny crop duster."

All of the victims survived and have been hospitalized and are under observation. Their symptoms range from moderate to severe, but all are expected to recover. The New Mexico State Police Investigations Bureau has interviewed the victims and witnesses. They have not confirmed the existence of a suspect at this time.

Ricin can be made in a home laboratory. Exposure to ricin in aerosol form can result in pulmonary edema, pneumonia, and respiratory failure. The onset of symptoms is usually within eight hours. Although the victims complained of eye irritation, no one suspected poisoning at the time, and all the students (continued on Page 7)

"Who made the connection?"

"Some guy called it in after he saw it on TV. He said he had seen the Tamara Gale interview and that when he saw the news report, the humming-bird description clicked for him. It seems he called Theresa Brewer at Channel 7 News, too. They're running with it like a tabloid freak show."

"Do you know who he is?"

"He said his name was Peter Riddle. We have the phone number logged. Why?"

"I don't know. I guess somebody would have noticed sooner or later." I mentally filed it as inter-esting: Who was this guy, and did it matter? *Riddle*? And do men even watch interviews with psychics?

CHAPTER 8

Thursday, October 27

Dave felt bad not mentioning the final clipping in his binder, the one with the headline MURDER IN SANTA MONICA CANYON—AGAIN! He wondered if Charlie knew how many bricks of gold were in that hole in the yard, and if he saw the piece, would he do the math?

He excused himself and went to the men's room. The bathroom walls were covered with jazz posters and blowups of album liner notes and critics' reviews. At the urinal, he was reading about Sonny Rollins when his phone rang. He fished his cell out of his pocket.

"Dave Putnam here."

"Dave, Robert van Evera." Van Evera was his boss, a captain. The Tamara Gale thing was turning into a PR nightmare for the LAPD. Theresa Brewer had a big audience and had been following the events since the Billy Taft story came out. In fact, she was the one who broke the story, which made Dave wonder who her source was. Van Evera wanted the buck to stop with Dave, but he knew it wouldn't; the circus was in town, and damage control was in order until the next thing came along to distract the media. "What have you got for me?"

Dave cleared his throat as he zipped up and finished reading. He hadn't known that Sonny Rollins lived three blocks from the World Trade Center when the towers went down and had been forced to bail out of his apartment with nothing but his sax.

"Putnam, godammit, say something!"

"Sorry, Cap. Frog in my throat. Interviewing a resource, as we speak."

"Well, I need to give a press report. Unless you want to do it."

"I'm allergic to hyenas, boss. We'll figure this out. There's bullshit all over this."

"And that's what you get paid for, sniffing out bullshit."

Occasionally, Dave thought, what looks like a gift turns out to be a curse. Tamara Gale was that kind of gift.

The Billy Taft case had been extremely frustrating. The kid was from Cheviot Hills, an affluent part of the West Side that never made the news, and lived with his father, who is a doctor, and step-mother—a much younger nurse; an *au pair* took care of Billy and his two small half-sisters. He was an A student, with no record of trouble, and was in AP classes so he could get a head start on college admissions.

The boy had last been seen walking away from school on a Thursday afternoon. He was supposed to have been at water polo practice but never showed up. His bike was still chained to the school's bike rack. When he didn't come home for dinner, his father started making calls. Billy's mother: his coach, his best friend—no one had heard from him. Worried by nine, anxious by ten, and extremely agitated at midnight, the father called nearby hospitals and then the police.

Dave had interviewed the family and found no sign of domestic problems, so he had written off runaway as a low probability. The au pair, an attractive twenty-something from Ireland, had been with the family for two years. She cleared, with no record and no known associates with questionable behavior, although Dave sensed that she was being a bit frugal with information. He sat with her for a moment, the two of them alone in the den. Dave knew that silence makes people with a secret uncomfortable. Finally, she cleared her throat and said, "I'm very fond of Billy, you know."

Dave waited.

"There's something his parents didn't know."

"Okay."

After a long examination of a spot of lint on her cashmere sleeve, the au pair finally said, "I found some magazines under his bed when I was cleaning his room."

"What kind of magazines?"

"Men's magazines."

Dave wasn't sure where this was going. *Playboy*? *Bodybuilder*? *Outdoor*? *GQ*? So what? "What kind—"

"Sex," she blurted out. "Men having sex with men."

An interview with the water polo coach revealed that Billy had missed practice every Thursday for the last month.

Four weeks later, with no leads, no ransom demand, and nothing to go on, Dave got a call from Tamara Gale. She said that she had read that he was the lead detective on the Billy Taft case, and that she had some information that might be useful. He asked her how she had come upon the information, and she said, "Not in a conventional manner."

"Okay, in what unconventional manner did you come up with information that might be useful to us?" Dave hated garbage calls like this—attention seekers, wannabe crime solvers, psychics, you name it—and didn't care if his thinly veiled sarcasm put this one off.

This was when she spouted the line that the papers had repeated about her "heightened faculties of awareness." Dave thanked her for her call and hung up.

Two days later Tamara Gale called again. This time she just said, "Blue jacket. He was wearing a blue jacket." That hadn't gone in the initial police report, or to the press, simply because neither the mother nor the au pair had thought of it until a week after the boy had gone missing. The mother, frantic that no progress was being made, had gone through his closet and realized that Billy's favorite blue jacket wasn't there, so she had called Dave with the update.

Dave drove to meet Tamara Gale at her house on Drexel Avenue in West Hollywood. It was a small but attractive Spanish bungalow, with a well-kept front yard entirely shaded by a large pepper tree. Ms. Gale greeted him at the door and shook his hand with a firm grip and a look of benevolent amusement, as if she knew but didn't care that he was irritated to be there.

She offered tea; he declined. They sat, and Dave pulled out a pen and notebook and looked at her with the pen poised. She still had the look: all-American girl, probably a cheerleader, maybe even a beauty pageant back in the day, but that day was over. What she had left was a certain poise, a self-assuredness that spoke of authority. Fine, Dave thought, she's sold on her own bullshit. A bullshit authority.

"Here's what I've seen," she told him. "And I can see it now." She closed her eyes. "I see a desert. I see a boy, and a hungry dog. There's an airplane. No, not an airplane, but propellers. More dogs. And the boy can't move. And there's a ski lift." She opened her eyes and said, "I'm afraid the boy has passed."

"Why would you think that?"

"My spirit guide informs me that the boy is sad."

Dave stood and thanked her. As he walked to his car, Tamara Gale said, "Don't discount what you don't understand."

Chapter 9

There's chatter from down on the street, a cacophony of barking, and now the clanging of feet on the stairs outside. I'm sitting in the kitchen trying to piece things together so they make sense, and interruptions can vaporize my train of thought. I've been jotting things down in a pocket notebook, which I hope to flesh out into a coherent narrative when the parts coalesce. *Wake up at Dave's. Repair body. Mindy conversations. Gold. Jimmy. Ratboy. Daniel visit. Dave at coffee shop. Tamara Gale, news clippings, her autobio.* Each has its own subentries.

A knock on the door makes me put down the notebook. I hear shuffling and giggling outside. A louder knock, and several more at the same time, on different parts of the door: trick-or-treaters, hard up for handouts if they're willing to hit up the residents of The Flora. I ponder the possibilities: what's the worst trick they can pull?

I wait them out and go back to my visit with Dave.

^

The mid-afternoon caffeine-jolt seekers were clearing out, so I got up and grabbed a real chair. It was quieter, and the music had changed to Art Pepper playing "Smack Up."

I was intrigued by Dave's little presentation, although I noticed there was another clipping in his folio, one that he was either saving for later or keeping to himself. I decided not to ask.

"I'll tell you what," I said. "I'll check out the book. You keep me in the loop. We'll see what happens. I've got a life to try to put back on track."

Dave smirked. He knew my life hadn't been on track for years. All he said was, "You want to tell me about that Saturn you're driving?"

I didn't. It belonged to a dead guy, and I had his ID. I figured it might come in handy one day.

When I got back to the apartment, Mindy was cleaning the kitchen. She had turned into quite the neat-freak lately, and I wondered whether this was a sign of maturity or an OCD response to anxiety. At some point she had found a bag of weed in the apartment, and, after hiding it for a while and smoking some of it in the bathroom, she finally started hitting Jason's little ceramic bong in front of me. As a former heroin addict, I was hard-pressed to come up with a rationale for hassling her, especially in my chronically befuddled state.

She came into the living room and gave me a hug.

"Hi, Dad. How was it out there?" She worried about me. And I was supposed to take care of *her*.

"Good, I guess. Dave's trying to suck me into playing cops and robbers. Otherwise, I navigated the real world without any disasters."

"Well, tell him to forget about it. You promised we could go to Hawaii."

"I did, didn't I? And we'll do that, I promise. But if we don't get you into school somehow, your mom's going to get her lawyer—"

"And what, sue for custody?"

She had a point. Allison already had custody and had booted Mindy out in a drunken rage.

"Look, Dad, I hate high school and don't want to go back. How about I test out and go to City College?"

"Now look—"

"And I'll get a job."

"We've got to—"

"And I'll stop smoking weed."

I caved. "Okay, you figure out the test-out process. I'll call your school so they stop sending your mom notices. Then we've got to figure out what we're going to do about money, the house, a place to live . . ." We'd been in limbo long enough. Jason's rent and utility bills were overdue, along with our cell phone bills. Our sanctuary was about to expire on us, and I didn't have a clue how to proceed. Whatever my friend Jimmy had planned for the gold, it wasn't happening anytime soon.

"One more thing," Mindy said. She went to the bedroom and came out with a battered briefcase that I hadn't seen before. "This was in the closet, behind some really nasty laundry." She opened it and showed me rows of neatly stacked bills—twenties and hundreds, mainly—wrapped in money bands. The yellow bands said "$1000," and there were eleven of them. I took two stacks of twenties and told her to put the rest back.

"There were a bunch of packets of meth, but I flushed them and took the baggies out to the trash."

CHAPTER 10

Thursday, October 27

Dave was feeling maxed out. Not only did he have Van Evera on his back, he also had a performance evaluation coming up.

There are two schools of thought about PEs: One says that they're ineffective, they don't paint an accurate picture of a cop's overall fitness to do the job, and that they're bad for morale. The other says that they are a useful management tool and help facilitate accountability and boost motivation. Dave knew that Van Evera was a micro-managing control freak that wanted every policy and procedure followed to the letter.

His previous PE had resulted in a determination of "Improvement Needed" and the initiation of a work performance program. It was the worst kind of bullshit, but fighting it was useless. A counselor had suggested that he attend AA meetings, as there was speculation that his PE outcome was related to his drinking. They couldn't mandate the meetings, but he went just to placate his reviewers.

His first experience was in a church in Culver City. He had gone in dreading the possibility that someone he knew might be there, let alone someone he had busted. Or, God forbid, a defense attorney, who could use his being there as a way of discrediting him in court. At the same time, he had a persistent vision of old men with missing teeth sitting around a table with a bare bulb hanging above it. The two scenarios were incongruous, and he had been pleasantly surprised to find them both baseless.

The group comprised about sixty men and women, cheerful, well dressed, and almost obnoxiously friendly. He hadn't shaken so many hands since his police academy graduation. He stocked up on cookies and coffee and took a seat in the back, ready to settle in and endure whatever the next hour and a half had to offer, but one of the happy handshakers, a guy named Milt, approached him and said, "This is where the sheep get picked off and the herd gets culled. C'mon up front with me."

The whole show was baffling. People singing "Happy Birthday," other people giving little speeches about gratitude. Apparently, they counted days and years of abstinence. A woman got up and introduced herself as Pam and, like the others, confessed that she was an alcoholic. Every time someone said that, everyone chimed in and said "Hi" to them.

Pam told a long story about drinking, drinking and driving, drinking and fighting, drinking and getting married. At one point she said that she divorced her husband—also a drunk—and then a year later married him again. When she deadpanned, "That's like taking a bite out of the same turd twice," the room burst into laughter, and Dave found himself laughing with them. She went on to tell how, after beating the crap out of her, the husband fell asleep masturbating on the living room sofa. She covered his balls in Krazy Glue and glued his hand to them. Then she called the police and passed out.

There was a lot of talk about steps and powerlessness and God that Dave couldn't decipher—it was as if they had their own language, some kind of in-group thing.

What Dave knew was that he didn't drink like Pam, but he was glad she had found AA, because it sounded like she needed it.

Chapter 11

Monday, October 31, night

It's quiet outside now. The trick-or-treaters have gone home, and only the occasional roar of a motorcycle or a broken muffler interrupts the calm. But it's early yet, and even though it's a Monday night, the street will soon yield its gift of trouble.

I feel like shit. I have two and a half Dilaudids left. They're 8 mg, so that's good. Plus a small amber vial of coke and a new bottle of Bacardi 151. There's also a Naloxone spray rig. I hit the last inch of the bottle of Jack I've been nursing. I can't piece together where it all came from or how this all started again.

My phone vibrates. It's been doing that, but I can't handle conversation right now. There's a syringe on the table. I can't remember where I got it, but it's time to use it.

^

I'm part of the new demographic of American junkies: pain-med addicts who, with the help of the pharmaceutical industry, the War on Drugs, and a predisposition to addiction, find themselves turning to Mexican heroin as a cheaper way to maintain a deal with the devil. When the DEA cracked down on the flow of synthetic opiates diverted from so-called legitimate channels, Mexican cartels flooded a hungry market with Afghan drugs that were an unintended consequence of the War on Terror.

When I submitted myself to treatment and went to Mexico, it was simply because the pain of continuing to use—with all its attendant results—was bigger than the payoff and I couldn't find my way out of the trap. The Second Chance at Life treatment center offered an unorthodox solution involving psychotropic drugs and a cleansing ritual that they claimed had an eighty-percent success rate. I was an anomaly: not only did I not get clean, I actually repressed the memory of the entire experience until fairly recently.

^

I point the syringe at the ceiling and tap it, then push the plunger until a drop of fluid appears at the needle's tip. Some people say it's a myth that a bit of air can cause problems, but I don't like the idea of bubbles in my veins. Which is funny, really: HIV, Hep C, prison—all major risks of addiction—plus losing my family and generally blowing up my life, and I'm worried about bubbles.

I'm a lightweight. I can still find a vein, and a half of one of the 8 mg tabs will keep me okay for a while. I've got to make what I have last until I can figure out what's going on. And that means filling in more of the gaps in my notebook while I wait for whatever is coming.

^

The day after Mindy gave me the money, I took care of our basics: phone bill, utilities, the rent.

The landlord at The Flora didn't ask about Ratboy; he was just happy to get cash. I didn't even have to touch the stacks in the yellow bands, which meant we still had eleven grand plus some pocket money in loose tens and twenties. On a whim, I grabbed a stack of hundreds and some twenties.

Then I started reading the book Dave gave me.

Tamara Gale claimed in her autobiography that she first met her "spirit guide" in 1965, when she was six years old and growing up in Bakersfield. The guide came to her in a vision. She was standing by the shore during a family day trip to Lake Webb when a woman approached her. The woman was dressed like a Persian princess, and when she reached Tamara, she knelt and took her hand and said, "You are a very special child, and I have much to teach you." Tamara replied, "You are so beautiful," and the woman disappeared. Tamara's brother, who was a year younger, asked her who she was talking to.

"There's no way to describe," I read, "the feeling that came over me, that I would be loved and protected throughout my life. It was a feeling I would have to summon for courage in later years when life handed me challenge after challenge."

I made a note at the time: *Lake Webb, 1965?*

^

According to my notes, Dave called me on Thursday.

"There's someone I want you to meet."

I had him on speakerphone. Mindy shook her head and swiped her fingertips across her throat.

"Who and why?"

"A guy named Jerry Ayres."

"Star Trek guy? He came back to life too?"

"No! Jesus, Charlie, it's another guy."

"So?"

"So he writes books on fake paranormal stuff. He wrote a review of Tamara Gale's book, and he's been poking fun at us for listening to her."

"Who's us?"

"LAPD. You read the clippings I showed you. We publicly acknowledged that she helped us."

"So why am I meeting him?"

"He's going to write another article, this time calling us out on listening to what he calls a manipulative phony. He's naming me as the prime chump in all this."

"Does he have an alternative theory of how she came up with the information?"

"That's just it. He says it wasn't new information. He told me to Google the Taft kid's name, and it turns out there's three different pictures of him and each time he's wearing a blue jacket. Then there's the fact that his parents have a condo in Rancho Mirage. It's not mentioned in the news reports, but if you check the dad's name you'll find the public record of ownership."

"So she did some research and then just guessed her way into it."

"Could be. But as it turned out, her guessing was better than our investigative work. Which makes me look bad."

"So what's all this got to do with me?" Mindy had been listening to the whole conversation and was making a gesture that looked like slamming an old phone down, although I don't know if she's ever used a landline in her life.

"Well . . ." I had to listen to some throat clearing and then a big sigh. "I was thinking maybe you could help me out and open his mind a bit to possibilities outside his paradigm, if you catch my drift."

"What? I should tell him I wake up with fatal bullet wounds to the head, and that I can fix them?" Mindy's looking at me like, *What the fuck?*

"Just help me out on this, okay?"

CHAPTER 12

Thursday, October 27

Dave loved being a cop, but it was getting to him. He blamed the job for his divorce, for his drinking, for the flab around his gut. He slept poorly and woke with a sense of dread. He had a thousand stories to tell, and now he had an agent, and he relished the idea of tapping out novels on a laptop in Sayulita, sticking to the occasional frosty Dos Equis. Retirement was only a few years out, but he didn't know if he could last that long or live on his benefits without having to move to Lancaster or Blythe, somewhere cheap and cheerless where washed-up cops and firefighters go to drink themselves into oblivion in run-down double-wides.

He pondered his golden parachute: the gold bricks nested in their case in the back of his closet. He had spent a lot of time thinking about them, spinning out scenarios about how to sell them, wash the money, live like it didn't exist so that nobody would know.

Meanwhile, the only option was to lie low. Follow this Tamara Gale thing wherever it went, hope that it blew over or got resolved somehow, or live with the consequences. That was pretty much his life philosophy: live with the consequences. On reflection, though, he had to admit that his real MO was to avoid consequences. But hell, who didn't do that? Shift blame, duck and dodge, wink here and fudge there; everybody was just trying to get a leg up.

Which wasn't to say it didn't get interesting.

CHAPTER 13

Friday, October 28

We met for dinner the next night. Mindy stayed home and prepped for the California High School Proficiency Examination. She had talked to a friend who had taken it and said the math was hard. Mindy's math is better than mine, so I'm not worried about it.

Dave's favorite dinner spot is a trendy dive in Santa Monica called Chez Jay. He told me once that their butter steak is juicier than Taylor Swift's underwear, which makes you wonder. About Dave, that is. The spot is right around the corner from the pier in what used to be a low-rent district, not far from where—back in the 60s—Chuck Dederich set up headquarters for Synanon, the original California junkie rehab program.

The neighborhood has changed, but Chez Jay has the continuity of a tortoise at the zoo. In the gloomy red light I made my way to the back, where I found Dave and a strange-looking man in a vintage, brown-checked tweed suit, complete with vest. He was tall and awkward looking, with black hairs that stuck out of ears that also stuck out. His face was too long, and his goatee didn't help. All that was missing was a deerstalker hat. His mouth was full of salad when Dave introduced us, but that didn't stop him from standing and saying, "Delighted to meet you" and trying to shake my hand with a fork in his.

After the waitress took my order, Dave polished off his drink, asked for another, and then said, "So check it out. Jerry here is a professional debunker of all things spooky—psychics, spoonbenders, telepaths, reincarnation; you name it, he'll rip it apart."

Jerry turned to me and, with a fresh mouth full of salad, said, "Do you know why there aren't more psychics that win the lottery?"

I told him no, but that it was a reasonable question.

"The same reason they don't have faith healers at hospitals." He grinned at me, showing big, horsey teeth with bits of green stuck to them. "I don't know if Dave told you, but my organization has a standing offer of one million dollars to anyone who can demonstrate any kind of psychic ability or paranormal event in a laboratory environment. That money's been on the table for a lot of years, and no one has claimed it yet."

Now that, I thought, would solve a lot of problems for me. But then I'd be a performing monkey on display. If Ayres had to pay out a million bucks, he was definitely going to make a lot of noise about it. I wondered who had stepped up and tried.

"So do you get any takers?"

"Sure. We get hustled all the time. I'd say that half of the participants are complete charlatans that are so used to pulling the wool over people's eyes that they think they can fool us in the lab. The other half are self-deluded and really believe they have special talents. They're disappointed when we demonstrate to them that they don't."

Dave popped a bite of steak in his mouth and said, "Jerry's also a stage magician. He knows all the tricks."

"Yes, well, there's that, and the fact that we use video monitoring and a number of other ways to catch cheats. Do you know the story of Clever Hans?"

I said I did not.

"In the 1890s, a German named Wilhelm von Osten claimed that his horse could do arithmetic. They would perform for crowds. Von Osten would ask the horse questions, including simple addition and subtraction, and the beast would tap the ground with his hoof. 'Amazing,' the crowds would say. 'Perplexing, but true,' claimed a panel of so-called experts. Hans gave consistently accurate answers, and the panel unanimously concluded that no trickery was involved."

"So the horse could do math?" With my recent experience, it was difficult to say anything was impossible, but I wasn't about to say so.

"Of course it could!" He picked at his teeth and glared at me. "And turkeys can write sonnets."

I'm not fond of sarcasm, except for my own. I waited while the waitress brought my food; I realized I was hungry and dug in.

"No, the horse could not count. He was responding to subliminal cues from his owner, who, without knowing it, would tense up until Hans got to the required number of foot taps. At that point, von Osten would relax just enough to signal the horse that it was time to stop."

"So he was a true believer."

"Yes. He was subject to what we call the observer-expectancy effect. And the protocols for demystifying the event weren't properly in place. We have the protocols to call bullshit on any and all claims of paranormal abilities."

"Who is 'we'?"

"We call ourselves ATOM—Advocating Truth Over Magic. We're an organization dedicated to bringing society out of the Dark Ages and showing that the true miracles are in the mundane: for example, a horse that interprets subtle human body language and responds to it. Particles rearranging themselves for fourteen billion years and arriving at this"—he gestured broadly—"incredible universe as it is right now, with us here discussing it."

Jerry was a weird guy, but I had to like him. At the same time, his certitude regarding things that can't be explained seemed a bit smug to me. He turned to Dave and said, "Your Tamara Gale, however, is simply a fraud. When I invited her to demonstrate her ability and collect a million bucks, you know what she said?"

Dave, now working on his new glass of Chivas, shook his head and flipped his hand in the air, a gesture I've never seen a sober person use.

"She said that the vibrations in my facility wouldn't be conducive to her communication, that her spirit guide connection was on a subtle plane and would be disrupted by my technical meddling. She even told me that my reductionist-materialist mindset was naive." Jerry looked down at his hands as if they surprised him, his head did an odd little quiver, and then he looked up at me. "Oh yes, and she said she didn't care about the money, that her gift was not for sale."

Dave looked irritated. He held up his hand for the waitress and waved his empty glass. We waited for his drink to arrive and for him to drain half of it before he said, "So how do you explain the poison drone?"

"I think that the specifics of her so-called vision during the interview are so vague that they could be matched—given some creative effort—to a variety of events. What did she say—a hummingbird and kids at a sports event? That could be any occurrence at any event in the world. A news helicopter reporting a foodborned outbreak at a baseball game. Bird flu takes a basketball team out of commission just before the championship game. Remember the observer-expectancy effect: if you believe in psychic abilities, then your expectation will interpret events to conform to a prediction. That's why the New Testament writers insisted that Jesus fulfilled the sayings of the prophets: they examined Old Testament prophesy and lined it up with what they had read and heard about the events of Jesus' life. It took a bit of imagination, but there was plenty of that going around at the time."

The guy had an answer for everything, it seemed, and enjoyed every minute of himself. He did, however, promise to hold off on his critique of the police, and he even waved for the check.

As if an afterthought, Jerry said, "We could have some fun Sunday night, you know."

Dave, mollified by the reprieve and the free meal, said, "How's that?"

Jerry pulled an American Express card out of his wallet. It must be an interesting line of work when you can write off taking a cop to dinner. He used a corner of the card to pick at a canine and said, "Your Tamara Gale. She's giving a performance right here in Santa Monica. Maybe we'll see some fireworks, eh?" Then he winked.

CHAPTER 14

Friday, October 28

Dave watched as the myth-busting magician lumbered toward the entrance to the restaurant. Between Ayres, who was a social moron, and Charlie, who was still a good bit off his game, Dave couldn't remember odder dinner company. But then Ayres was a sly one, and it could be that his ineptness was a ruse.

Dave had another drink coming, and an improvised plan for rest of the evening. But the drink, on top of the previous drinks, was the one that shot him past the mark and into the zone where clear thinking required effort. So did walking, as he found out when he almost slid on the sawdust floor on his way past the cash register.

The night air helped a bit.

Jerry Ayres had something up his sleeve. And whatever trick he was about to deliver, he wanted Dave there to see it. For Ayres, this was mortal combat, and Tamara Gale was the enemy.

^

The Billy Taft murder never got solved, even though they found the body. Some of the other detectives ribbed Dave about his "new psychic girlfriend," but the case ran cold and the media moved on.

Then, four months later, Kyle Johnson disappeared. As a habitual runaway—twice from expensive residential treatment programs—he wasn't about to get top billing for an investigation, but his dad went public and LAPD stepped it up. And then Dave got the call from Tamara Gale.

"That poor boy. He's caught in the gray zone between worlds, crying out for help."

"I didn't know you could get help in the gray zone." Dave just couldn't resist.

"His spirit can't move on until he gets justice."

"Okay, great. Got any propellers and ski lifts for me? A boulder or two?"

"Your skepticism has already been noted, Detective Putnam. But yes, the boy has reached out, and my guide heard him. And yes, boulders, stretching out into the ocean. A tunnel."

"That's it?"

"I hope it's enough. Goodbye, Detective."

Dave drove to the Venice pier parking lot at the end of Washington Boulevard and backed into a spot between a van and an SUV so he could have some privacy, even though there was no one around. He opened his trunk and unzipped the duffel bag that was nestled between a bucket and some fishing gear and a camping tent he hadn't used in a long time. He decided a nip would be helpful and took a few big hits from the bottle of Seagram's he had in the bag. Trading his sports coat for a battered army jacket, and putting on an old blue watch cap, he took the Desert Eagle out of the bag and placed it in the bucket under some rags. Holding on to it for all this time had been insane. Gift or no gift, it had been a liability for too long. He pulled out his Goture telescopic rod and locked it into full extension. He missed fishing, but tonight wasn't the night for it. And the days were long gone that he would eat anything from Santa Monica Bay.

He had just closed his trunk when he saw two guys come around from the far side of the van. Tweakers, and probably not just looking for a handout. He shifted the pole to his left hand, along with the bucket.

"Hey, gonna go catch a few?" Tall, skinny, scraggly beard. Greasy hair and a tic, like there was a short circuit in the nerve in his right cheek. He put himself in front of Dave while the other, shorter guy moved to flank Dave's left side; he had a Bowie knife that he tapped against his thigh. Big Tweaker and Little Tweaker, smirking and twitching, ticcing and tapping. Dave knew the type from his days in Narcotics. If they had ever had any smarts or scruples, they were long since washed out in both accounts. He held up his hand and said, "Whoa, easy," and backed around to between his car and the SUV. They both followed.

Big Tweaker said, "You got some help for a brother?" Dave's shield was in his wallet. No way was he giving it up to these dipshits.

"Yo, yo, check it out," he said. "You want to get high?"

"No, man, I want your wallet, s'what I want."

"I know a bitch that's got fuckin' bags of glass, like five minutes from here. She'll get us all high and y'all can party with her."

"You're full of shit. What's her name?"

There, a buy signal. "Connie. She's at the Beachside, right up the street. Want to talk to her?" Little Tweaker's knife was doing a drum roll on his pant leg, but the tall guy was licking his lips and doing some crazy-eyed calculating.

"Pull her up on your phone and give it to me."

Dave got his phone out of his pocket and selected his sister Connie's name from the contacts list and showed it to them; then he tossed the phone to the tweaker with the knife. In the same movement, he grabbed the Desert Eagle and put it in the guy's face.

"Hey, dude, what the fuck? It's cool, hey, fuck—" Big Tweaker's tic was freaking out, and his right hand went up of its own accord to his head and started slapping it. Little Tweaker, having dropped both the phone and the knife, stood immobilized but hostile. Dave thought through his options. They all sucked.

"My phone." The short guy picked it up and handed it back to Dave.

"So here's what we're gonna do." He had made a decision. It was sketchy, but the whole scene was fucked up already. "You boys are gonna walk down the beach toward the water."

"What—" the big one started. Dave showed him the big hole at the end of his gun and said, "And you're both gonna shut the fuck up."

When they got near the water he said, "Okay, here's the fun part. Take off your clothes. No talking." He watched them strip, but looked away when Big Tweaker dropped his pants. For some reason, the fool had a hard-on. Dave shook his head and said, "Okay, gentlemen. I hope you like the water. Move!"

They walked out to their ankles and stopped.

"Keep going until you have to tread water. And then stay there until I'm gone. Got it?"

They both nodded, shivering now, and lurched out into the waves. Dave went back to the spot where they had undressed, wiped off the Desert Eagle, and put it in the pile of clothes. He was pretty sure the gun would get traded for some crystal meth in the next half hour, and then it would probably move up the connection ladder once or twice. That would give him enough degrees of separation for comfort. He was also confident that these guys were too dumb to have noticed what kind of car he drove.

Neat, really. Life imitating art. In his novel, which was already on his new agent's desk, he had written the scene as a carjacking. He wondered if he'd have to take it out.

CHAPTER 15

Monday, October 31, night

There is a Pavlovian pre-high to injecting opiates. The anticipation of relief is in itself relief. I depress the plunger and wait. It doesn't take long.

The mind wanders . . .

^

I should stay alert. Well, it's too late now. Where did I even get the idea that there's another bullet headed my way? My phone vibrates again. The answer is probably there, in a text message, or a voicemail, but who gives a shit?

I mean really.

There is nothing but this moment, and this moment is just fine.

^

Some time has gone by. The last thing I remember is that second, right before my forehead hit the table and I thought, not for the first time, "Fuck, am I gonna die?"

Now I remember why I like getting high. There's a lot to say for the state of pure euphoria, unmolested by the relentless gabble and chatter of my mind.

More time goes by, and I emerge from my perfect cocoon at the center of a hostile universe. My chest itches, and scratching it is immensely satisfying.

I drag myself out of the kitchen and fall into the beanbag chair. The blowfish lamp spins lazily, its mouth obscene like a sex doll's.

As an experiment, I leave the body.

^

The first time I roamed—during my botched heroin treatment in a clinic somewhere south of Juarez—I was crazy-high on ibogaine and whatever else was in the brew they fed me. Instead of the intended "deep, therapeutic, and sacramental rite of passage," I had some sort of seizure and ditched my body for a bird's-eye view of the scene: a dark and smoky room filled with people, drums and chanting, my body lying face-up on a mat.

A year later, when I got shot in the head while riding a bicycle, I woke up looking down at my own dead body and somehow got pulled back into it. At first it felt cumbersome, but I got used to making it work. Later, I even learned how to repair it. Meanwhile, I've been able to come and go as I please, although Daniel—who for some reason knows about these things—told me that I had to be careful about a few things: don't roam too far or for too long. I've tried both and didn't like the results.

^

The body by itself is a useless thing, like a car without a driver. I gaze down at it from the blowfish's point of view; it sprawls peacefully in the beanbag chair under the dim glow of the lamp. It could be asleep, OD'd, or dead again, but I can always fix it.

I drift outside. The door is not a noticeable obstruction, but there's an interesting point if I pass through sideways where I can see both inside and outdoors at the same time. From the second-floor landing I study the empty street, which is lined on both sides with battered cars that were new two decades ago. The few recent models are conspicuous, and as I watch I see a kid walk briskly toward one, looking over his shoulder as he gets in. Copping dope is the easy guess here.

One of the newer cars is a gray Nissan Rogue parked across the street, with a man sitting in it. He's smoking a cigarette. When he looks up at me, I'm startled, but then I realize he can't see me. I also realize I've seen him—and the car—before, but I can't pin it down. I think he's waiting for me to come out.

I see him check his watch.

CHAPTER 16

Monday, October 31, night

I wish I had a gun.

I wish I knew who is down there, and why.

I wish I knew why I don't know who it is, and what he's waiting for. I feel like I should know, but I can't access the memory. Is it because I did a faulty repair? Or did something happen that broke my access mechanism? My brain has never been a very reliable instrument, but this is a whole new level of malfunction.

As my high fades, I look at my notes: *Wake up at Dave's. Repair body. Mindy conversations. Gold. Jimmy. Ratboy. Daniel visit. Dave at coffee shop. Tamara Gale, news clippings, her autobio.* I add two entries: *Dinner w/Dave & fraudbuster Jerry Ayres. Tamara Gale performance?*

Under *Tamara Gale, autobio,* there's a subheading that says *Lake Webb, 1965?* I ignore the messages on my phone but use it to Google *Lake Webb.* I had gone there with Allison and Mindy once, on a road trip back when things were still good. We rented a sailboat and drifted around on a windless July afternoon. I remember reading about it at the time. Now a Wikipedia entry confirms that Lake Webb didn't exist until 1973, eight years after Tamara Gale claimed to have met her Persian princess there. It had been created out of the lake bed of the former Buena Vista Lake, which had dried up after the creation of the Isabella Dam.

Tamara Gale Performance rings a bell.

71

^

Two nights after we had dinner at Chez Jay, I met Dave and Jerry at a theater on Wilshire in Santa Monica. The tickets cost forty dollars, so I had to pony up two of Ratboy's twenties.

A camera crew was set up at the rear of the theater. The crowd was mainly women, a few with boyfriends or husbands. Some carried copies of Tamara's autobiography, presumably for signing. We were an anomaly: three males, one dressed like an eccentric academic, one clearly a cop, and me in jeans and a flannel shirt over a tee—it was the day that the weather had turned.

When the lights dimmed, a man walked up to the microphone and introduced himself as Philip Gale. He looked like an aging 80s TV star: blond, bland, and going soft. There was an interesting scar on his forehead, but otherwise his face was smooth as a baby's. His red sweater was an odd choice, but his vintage lime-green Hush Puppies made me want to like him.

"Thank you for joining us here tonight. Who here is new to Tamara's work?"

Only a few hands went up.

"We live in the Scientific Age, and yet there is so much left unexplained. Here, let me read to you from a recent article on consciousness from a respected scientific journal." He put on a pair of reading glasses and produced an index card that he moved back and forth until it was the right distance. "It's called *Consciousness Emerges*, and here's what it tells us: 'Somewhere along a tangled path, sights, sounds and insights pop into awareness.' Wow! C'mon, is that the best you got? So far, science trying to explain consciousness is like a dog trying to explain an Escher drawing." Chuckles from the audience; a groan from Jerry.

"Some experts"—he made quote signs in the air—"go so far as to say that consciousness is an illusion, an accidental byproduct of biochemical processes occurring in our brains. But the wisdom of the ancients and the most advanced theories of quantum physics are now converging to reveal that consciousness is the fundamental reality, one that gives rise to the material world, including biochemical processes. In fact, a better description of the world would be *Physical Reality Emerges*. And so, what you'll experience tonight—even though it will seem mysterious and perhaps hard to believe— is perfectly consistent with a practical, day-to-day view of life, as well as with cutting-edge science. We ask only that you open your minds and hearts to the larger truth of love and deep connection." He turned to his right and put out his hand. "And now I am proud to introduce my lovely wife, Tamara Gale!"

The applause was instant, the clapping quick and chirpy. When it died down, Jerry leaned toward me and, in a stage whisper, said, "This ought to be rich."

Tamara Gale stepped out from the curtains and glided toward her husband, stopping halfway to turn to the audience and spread her arms as if she were the Pope himself—no weakness here—and drank up the new applause and cheering before moving to her husband and embracing him. She wore a pantsuit that almost matched his Hush Puppies, and had a wireless microphone pinned to her lapel. Her husband walked offstage and she motioned for silence.

"The good news," she said, her voice rich on the mic, "is that our gathering together here is consecrated—dedicated to the sacred purpose of deepening our connection with God and each other, of tapping into the vein of gold that runs through us all, of sipping from the well of Spirit so that our deepest thirst is quenched." She gazed out at us, sweeping the room with a calculated authority, a look that said *I know you*, and then shouted, "SO WHO'S THIRSTY?"

Jerry didn't bother whispering this time, but broke the silence and said, "I could use a drink right about now."

There were a few nervous titters around the room. Tamara Gale zeroed in on Jerry and gave a beauty-pageant smile. "Hello, Jerry. I believe you can buy one right next door, but then you might miss an opportunity to have your oh-so-scientific mind blown." Now the laughter was general and hearty. "So, what brings you here tonight? Oh, wait"—she put the back of her hand to her forehead, mocking a carnival medium, and closed her eyes—"I see an article in your favorite magazine, *The Modern Skeptic*. Another exposé to keep the citizens informed." She opened her eyes and flashed the smile again. "And look—my favorite policeman, Dave Putnam. I'll tell you what. Bear with me, and I'll buy you both that drink later."

There was an armchair on stage next to the microphone stand. Tamara made a show of lowering herself into it while at the same time extending her hands, palms up, toward the audience. "And now," she said, "let us begin."

A deep Tibetan gong sounded over the speakers, reverberating throughout the room, shimmering as it gradually faded. Tamara's voice broke through the shimmer with an invocation: "I call upon you, O Mandana, to fill me with your presence and speak through me."

The gong rang again, and again. At each successive ring, Tamara's expression changed slightly; her gaze became more penetrating, and her hands, still palms up, moved outward as if she were holding an expanding, invisible globe. At the final ring, she placed her palms together and brought her hands up so that her fingertips touched her chin. The house lights went fully dark and a spotlight focused on Tamara. When the gong finally faded, she spoke.

"I am here." The voice was a full octave lower than Tamara's natural voice, and oddly inflected. The woman seated to my left gasped, and Jerry, on my right, started to let out a snort but managed to contain it.

^

Sitting here, now, feeling like shit and waiting for trouble, I remember the voice. "I am here." Ominous. Portentous. Ridiculous. Impressive. It was like tearing up at a Disney movie and knowing your emotions are being played by hokum, but admiring the effectiveness of the manipulation.

Then it pops into my head that I sent Mindy away.

Because something bad is going to happen.

CHAPTER 17

Dave liked the sound of the gong. It was soothing, and it meshed with the few drinks he'd had in the parking lot so that now he was in that perfect dreamy zone where everything was just fine. *Show me what you got.*

He studied Tamara's face. It had transformed, in stages, with each strike of the gong. She had at first looked serene, and he could see the corn-fed beauty queen that she claimed in her book to have been. At each new ringing tone her expression changed, becoming more severe, eyes hooded, focused, challenging. When the spotlight snapped on he was jolted by the sensation that she was looking right at him—into him, as if knowing his thoughts.

A new voice came over the speakers, low and modulated, commanding and personal: "I am here."

To his left, Jerry's barely repressed grunt of contempt seemed inappropriate, like a belch during wedding vows. He elbowed Jerry and gave a slight shake of his head.

The new voice continued: "Welcome, my friends. I am pleased to visit with you, and grateful to Tamara for serving as a portal to your existential plane. I know you have questions—who would like to begin?"

There was a nervous rustling, whispers, and then a hand went up.

"Stand, so we may all see you."

A large woman in a floral-print caftan rose from her seat and said, "Where are you?"

Tamara raised her right hand and gestured toward the audience. "I am here with you, and I am in my own world at the same time."

"What is your world like?" the woman asked.

"My world is the world of your favorite dreams. We are forever young, even though we are very old. Our language has no antonym for the word love. As I read your life in the Akashic record, I see that you will join us in due time and you will see for yourself."

The woman remained standing, seeming to have more on her mind. Dave wondered if she was contemplating asking what "in due time" meant. She finally sat down.

Tamara—or *Mandana*—gazed around the room. When she spoke, her words were separated by long spaces. "I . . . see . . . someone . . . who . . . is . . . suffering."

Dave heard Jerry whisper, "Oh boy, here we go."

"Your husband is very sick." She scanned the first few rows and then looked up to the ceiling as if an answer to an unspoken question were coming to her. Then she looked back down at the audience and zeroed in on a woman several seats in front and to the left of where Dave was sitting.

He watched the woman stand up hesitantly, a nice-looking woman in her forties, expensively dressed, trembling, her eyes brimming.

The deep voice spoke softly now. "It is time to release your husband, even though he seems to be still alive. I see him in his hospital bed, connected to machines, but he has already joined us in my world."

The woman let out a plaintive "Oh no" and then collapsed into her seat and burst into tears.

"I know you are very sad," the voice continued. "Where I live, there is no sadness, but it is part of your human experience. He will speak to you tonight, in your dreams, and he will tell you that he is at peace."

"Fucking bitch," Jerry whispered. "Somehow, she did research on audience members, or it's being fed to her. I'll bet you a thousand dollars she's wearing an earpiece."

The woman sobbed for a moment and then took a deep breath and got her act together. After a brief pause, Tamara/Mandana began again.

"Life in its fullness brings us joy and grief, anger and laughter, waking and sleeping—Ah! I see someone who struggles to find sleep." Again, she surveyed the audience, stopping when she found her target somewhere in the back row.

"Sleep is the world you visit that lies between your dimension and mine. It is perfectly real—your spirit goes there and has experiences just like it has when you are awake. Because you cannot remember them fully and accurately, the dream world seems different from this one. When you have trouble getting to sleep—or staying asleep—it is the spirit's reluctance to enter the dream dimension that is the problem. Pills will not help you. I have brought you a gift, through Tamara, that will guide you to sleep. She will tell you about it later."

"Check it out," Jerry said in Dave's ear. "They'll be selling sleep CDs and MP3s. Statistically speaking, about half the audience is likely to have sleep issues."

Chapter 18

Sunday, October 30

Tamara was talking about sleep. On a whim, I put my body to sleep and roamed.

There was nothing interesting in the lobby, or even backstage. Then I found a red door with a sign that said *Cast Only* on it. I passed through and saw Tamara Gale's husband sitting at a table with an open laptop in front of him. He had a headset on and was reading instructions from the screen. Then he spoke into the microphone: "Woman in fourth row, right from center, red hair, black silk blouse."

I hovered behind him and watched the screen. It was split, showing on one side a view of the audience from a corner of the stage and a Word document on the other. He read from the document: "Needs a hip operation. Flight attendant. Fourteen months into worker's comp dispute. Claims emergency exit training injury." He hit a key, and the view switched to a front-seat view of Tamara in her chair.

Tamara put her hand to her temple and said, "Someone here is in pain when she walks."

I went back to my body, which had tilted toward Jerry in an apparent nap. When I took my head off his shoulder he said, "Watch this. Classic—she's fishing. Then she'll add details and—"

I interrupted him and said, "She's got an earpiece. Her husband's feeding her lines from off-stage. He's reading from a document."

He turned to me and said, "And how do you know this?"

I shrugged and said, "You should go back there and check it out." I told him where the dressing room was and watched him make his way to the aisle.

CHAPTER 19

Sunday, October 30

Dave had always had sleep problems. He couldn't get to sleep; he couldn't stay asleep. He'd tried Ambien, Lunesta, melatonin, and a variety of internet miracle cures that left him brain-dead the following day. One time he got home from work at midnight and had a few drinks, then he took an Ambien and went to bed. The next thing he knew, he was driving up Topanga Canyon with his gun in his lap.

He wondered if Jerry was right—that Tamara Gale would be selling sleep gimmicks in the lobby after the show. Too bad that it was all a hustle. There was something compelling, tantalizing even, about the whole performance. Regardless, nothing so far was helpful in trying to figure out how Tamara had come up with the information she had fed him about the boys' murders, or about the incident in New Mexico.

He checked his watch. One thing he was sure of: it was time for a drink. He knew, on some level, that this was problematic. In the past, he had made use of a flask for times like this, but it had seemed too desperate a measure, proof that there was something wrong that he didn't want to deal with.

The strange voice from the stage continued. "Tell me, dear child, do your dreams frighten you?"

Dave turned in his seat and looked back at the target, a young woman, pale and thin to the point that he wondered if she was a drug user. Her left arm was tattooed to the wrist, but Dave knew that that was no longer the signifier that it might once have been.

The young woman stood and cleared her throat but didn't say anything.

Tamara said, "Your sadness follows you to the dream world. When you pray at night, I will send you guidance for crossing over. When you awaken, you will have new eyes."

The woman sat, and Tamara's gaze hovered over the audience. She put her fingertips to her temple and said, "Someone here is in pain when she walks."

Jerry said something Dave couldn't hear. He glanced over and saw Charlie whispering something in Jerry's ear. They had a brief exchange, and then Jerry got up and threaded his way past the people in their row and walked toward the exit. Dave was finding Jerry to be irritating, a smug Mr. Know-it-all. He turned his attention back to Tamara onstage.

"I see traveling, in the sky. A fall. You can't have fallen out of the sky . . . hmmm. Yes, you were practicing, learning how to help people, and now you need an operation. Your leg. No. Your hip."

A woman in the front row stood and said, "How could you know that?"

"All is recorded, and much is available for me to see. Your spirit's vibrations are like a unique code that takes me to your entry in the Akashic record. I see that you have lived in many places. In your most recent past life you were a healer, but now you must place your faith in doctors. And yet I see that there is resistance to your getting help."

"Yes. My company doesn't think my accident caused my hip problem. They're saying—"

Suddenly Jerry's voice boomed out from the rear of the auditorium.

"Do you deny you are wearing a headset?"

Tamara raised her attention to the back of the theater. Her eyes seemed to deepen in her skull, her shoulders hunched, and her voice came out in a guttural hiss. "You . . . have . . . no . . . standing . . . here."

The spell in the room, rather than being broken, was heightened. Dave was both fascinated and furious. Jerry making a spectacle of himself while with Dave would make them both part of a story that would make him—and the PD—look bad.

"That doesn't answer my question," Jerry said. "I have an interesting file on you and your husband, and tomorrow I'm going to release it on my website and my podcast. For the rest of you, let's just say that there's a riddle involved, and we're going to solve it."

Tamara's manner and tone reverted to Mandana in conciliatory mode.

"I am not your enemy, Jeremy Ayres, nor are you mine. I have conferred with your guardian in the past, and shall do so again, in the hope of loosening the grip that fear of the unknown has on you. Now I say to you all, goodbye." With that, her shoulders straightened, her countenance changed, and—Dave could only surmise—the Mandana personality, whatever it was, left Tamara.

Now she stood and spread her arms again, embracing the audience.

"I wish to thank you for your presence, which is sacred to me. I am honored to stand before you and offer myself as a conduit for Mandana's magnificent presence and wisdom. All things happen in this universe for a reason, including—"

Suddenly, Tamara swayed, as if she had been buffeted by a high wind. She held up her hands, seemingly trying to ward off a threat that only she could see. Her face twisted into one of distress and a moaning sound filled the room.

"Ohhhh . . . so much pain," she wailed.

Dave watched, fascinated, and then turned back to Jerry, still at the top of the aisle, who shrugged and shook his head.

Tamara straightened and regained her composure. "I am receiving," she said, "a horrible vision. I see . . . signs . . . signs of death. Many people will die, and more will know great pain. An explosion, here, in this city. Oh my God—" She swayed again, almost falling sideways, and then recovered. "Horrible. I'm so sorry. Horrible." And then she collapsed on the stage.

Chapter 20

I sent Mindy away because there was a threat. Who made it? I know the memories are there, somewhere, but access is the problem. It's like having a library full of books but no indexing system.

It would be nice to take another hit right about now, but I'm pretty sure that I'm going to need it more as the night plays out. Not that rationing dope has ever been my strong suit; I've just got a feeling. And, I need to clear my head.

There's coffee in the kitchen. It's been there for a few hours, but it's hot and should be okay with a big dose of creamer. I fix it up and sit at the kitchen table. The coffee is strong and sweet, and it makes me feel better. Just a little.

It's time to fill in some blanks. I don't think I'm going to like it. First, I roam out to the landing.

The Nissan is still there. The guy's talking on a cell phone.

Okay, fuck it.

I go back to the body, which I've left seemingly asleep at the table. My phone is waiting for me there. I wake the body and then I wake the phone and check my texts.

The first one is Mindy, dated October 31 at 2 a.m. *Dad, it's late. Where are you?* So I lost a day. Bad enough that I've had to piece together the last month.

2:26 a.m. *Dad, what's going on? I'm worried.*

10:02 a.m. *Dad. What the fuck? This is not cool. What am I, your mom?*

10:44 a.m. *Charlie, Dave here. Where are you? Last I saw, you were with Zombie girl. Please tell me you didn't go home with her. Call your daughter, for Christ's sake.*

11:58 a.m. *Charlie, Dave. Where the fuck are you? Anyway, I have to go to the school in New Mexico, see if I can interview the kids. Maybe somebody noticed something.*

After each one, a robotic voice says, *End of message. To replay, press 1* . . . I hit 7 to delete. There are more, but something's coming back to me.

Zombie girl. Now that rings a bell.

Sunday, October 30

After Tamara Gale delivered her performance, people sat frozen in their seats while her husband rushed out and knelt by her unmoving form. He put his hand to her throat, then his ear to her lips, and then signaled to the audience with his other hand, five fingers, palm out, and then a thumbs-up. He started to get up but then, thinking better of it, leaned down to her clip mic and said, "She's fine. The power of her vision overwhelmed her. Please, everybody, relax, and thank you for joining us tonight."

A nervous chatter picked up as people stood and filed out toward the exits. Dave got up and glared at Jerry, shaking his head. On our way out, I caught a glimpse of a really odd creature packing up the video gear.

She was easily six feet tall, pageboy haircut streaked with purple, eyebrows pierced with silver snake rings, and her earlobes stretched and embedded with amber disks the size of quarters. Her right arm had a snake tattoo coiled around it, ending in a fanged open mouth at the top of her hand. She seemed to catch my eye as we passed.

A junkie knows a junkie, anywhere.

There was a restaurant with a bar adjoining the theater lobby. Dave made a beeline for the bar, shouldering his way through the pack, and Jerry and I followed. I noticed a tremor in Dave's hand as he motioned for the bartender.

Three double shots of Chivas Regal appeared on the bar. Dave slapped down a fifty.

The last time I had a drink or a drug was when a client—the one who got me killed twice—seduced me in order to retrieve a document that was at the center of her screwball case. Neither alcohol nor weed nor the two roofies she slipped in my drink had any effect on me. The time before that, I banged a decent hit of Jimmy's heroin, also with no result. But that was after I got a bullet in my brain and before my experience with self-repair, and I had no idea what my Twilight Zone metabolism would do with intoxicants now. I took a sip and it felt good going down.

Dave took more than a sip and then looked at his empty glass as if something strange had happened. His hand went up for another as he said to Jerry, "So what was that all about?"

Jerry sniffed at his drink and put it back on the bar. "Charlie, apparently on a hunch, suggested I have a look in the dressing room. And what do you suppose I see when I go there?" He seemed highly pleased with himself.

"Humor me," Dave said, surly, and clearly not happy with the turn of events.

Jerry put his hand, palm out, to his forehead, like Tamara had. "I see a very deceitful husband with a laptop, reading an audience member's private medical data into a microphone."

"So she's entirely a fraud."

"Of course she's entirely a fraud. Look, she knows about our standing offer. I already told you what she said to me about it, but check out what she wrote in her book."

I was curious about this myself—how could she publicly justify not taking a challenge that would not only pay her a million bucks but would vindicate her in the eyes of her detractors? And how could her followers not wonder? I had another— larger—taste of my drink and said, "Okay, do tell."

"She wrote that her guide would be shy in a test environment. The video and electronic gear and the 'overall negative vibrational aspect' are 'counterproductive to her transdimensional connection.' How's that for some serious bullshit? And her fans buy it." He gave an elaborate roll of his eyes.

Dave said, "So how do you explain her information on my cases?"

"I don't know, but I'm going to find out. First off, tomorrow I'm going to blow Tamara Gale up on my podcast. I already had a story ready, but tonight put the cherry on top."

I suddenly remembered something I had marked as strange. "You know, I read some of her book and something jumped out at me." The bar was now three deep in patrons, mainly women from the show. An arm reached past me to grab a Heineken from the bartender; it had a snake coiled around it and seemed to go on forever. I turned and looked her up and down. She was a mile and a half of legs and way too much neck, like there was some giraffe in her DNA, but weirdly hot anyway. Now that we were up close, I could see there was a tattoo on her neck: in tall, narrow, inch-high script were the numerals 5150. She was clearly high. We locked eyes, and she nodded and then tilted her head toward the rear exit. Then the snake whisked the Heineken away. Now it was Dave's turn to roll his eyes as he said, "Whew! Zombie girl. I think she likes you."

Jerry said, "Yes, it does appear so. Now, what was it you read?"

I tried to recall the details. I had finished my drink and was feeling a nice buzz. It seemed like another one would be fun. Dave noticed and motioned for the bartender.

A lake—it was something about a lake. Then it came to me.

"Okay, look . . . She talks about when she first met her Persian princess spirit guide—what's her name? Oh yeah, Mandana—and says that it was at Lake Webb in 1965. I was up there once, and I remember reading about how Lake Webb was created in 1973, eight years later. There was no lake there in 1965—it was the dry bed of what used to be Buena Vista Lake, which had dried up when they made the Isabella Dam."

Jerry liked this enough to finally pick up his drink and make a dent in it. "I suspect," he said, "that a good deal of her personal history is contrived. I just haven't put the resources into investigating it. Bravo to that discovery, though. I'll definitely use it." He held up his glass in a toast. Out of the corner of my eye, I saw Ms. 5150 tilting her beer at me from the end of the bar by the restrooms.

Dave retrieved our fresh drinks from the bar, handing me mine, and then he turned to Jerry and said, "Look. You've got plenty of material for tomorrow. Just leave me out of it, okay? Give me a few days to do a background check on her and her husband. I'll run them through NCIC and give you anything I find, but you can't reveal me as the source."

Jerry stroked his goatee and contemplated the offer. Finally he said, "I can do that, but there's definitely something off about her revelations to your department, and I intend to find it and expose it."

They toasted to their agreement and then knocked back their drinks.

I tossed mine down, burning my throat, and excused myself.

CHAPTER 21

Sunday, October 30

Dave watched Charlie leave and said, "I can't believe he's going after that." He was feeling pretty good now. The heat was off. Jerry had promised him a few days, and Dave knew that if he had some time to get to the bottom of all this, he could deflect any attention Jerry tried to steer toward the department. Van Evera would be breathing down his neck, but Dave would handle it. And besides, the drinks had kicked in, and the two of them were swimming in a sea of well-dressed females.

Jerry seemed to have a low tolerance for alcohol. He burped audibly and didn't seem to care or even notice; he tugged at his goatee and yawned, then burped again. Then he turned to Dave and poked his finger at him, saying, "You know that bit Charlie brought up about the reference to Lake Webb in her book? I'm thinking the whole thing is a crock of shit. Not just the goofy clairvoyant scam, but the whole story. This tale gets wackier and more fun all the time. Anyway, I've got her whole story right here." He tapped his herringbone jacket's breast pocket.

Dave was starting to like Jerry, his eccentric new pal. And Charlie, of course. Charlie was a comrade-in-arms; what they had been through defied explanation. Even though they had worked together in the past, Dave hadn't really known the man. And now he was a friend.

"Dave—" He snapped out of his reverie and saw Jerry looking at him quizzically, head cocked to one side. "You okay?"

"Hell yeah, I'm more than okay." He gave Jerry a hearty slap on the shoulder. "Wackier and more fun, you bet. You know what I think?"

"What's that?"

Dave had forgotten what it was that he had thought. Maybe there had been no thought there at all, as if the question were a placeholder conjured to last until a real thought arose. Fortunately, he didn't have to come up with one, as his phone chirped and vibrated in his pocket.

He looked at the phone. Why would Van Evera be calling him now? He excused himself and walked toward the restroom as he swiped the phone to answer.

"Putnam!" There was nothing friendly about the tone.

"Yes, sir. Rather late. What's up?" He had a sense that he was being a bit informal, but fuck it, he was off duty and it was ten at night.

"Rather late what's up? What the fuck, Putnam? I own you, it's never late, and I'll tell you what's up."

"Okay, I'm all ears." Dave wasn't in the mood for Van Evera's surly bullshit.

"You're going to New Mexico."

"For real? What's up with that?"

"One of the kids in that aerosol poisoning case just died. That turns it into a murder investigation and ties it into ours. You seeing the picture here?"

Dave's head cleared a little as he saw the implications. "Yeah, our Tamara Gale is the common denominator."

"Our Tamara Gale? Make that *your* Tamara Gale."

And there it was. Her name would be in the news again, and the media would be all over the department. He decided to tell his boss what he had just seen. When he got to the part about Jerry Ayers threat to expose Tamara Gale, Van Evera just said, "Jesus fucking Christ."

"It gets worse. You ready?"

"What do you mean, it gets worse? How the fuck can it get worse?"

Dave described Tamara's bizarre performance and hysterical prediction at the end of her show.

"An explosion? Here? She's so full of shit it makes me tired."

"Theresa Brewer was there."

"Shit."

"So don't be surprised if her whole act is on the news tomorrow."

"Jesus fucking Christ."

"Yep."

"You're still going to New Mexico. Interview the survivors, anyone at the event that might have seen something or someone out of the usual. You're flying out of LAX, Southwest Airlines, first thing in the morning. I'm texting you the reservation."

Dave used the restroom and then went back to the bar, sober as the pope and pissed about it. He found Jerry arguing with three women from the show, saying, "You don't think it's weird that Tamara's *guide*"—here he made ostentatious air quotes—"happens to be named *Mandana*?" Dave tapped him on the shoulder and said, "I gotta go."

CHAPTER 22

Sunday, October 30

Her name was Zinia. She said people called her Zini, but I should call her Z. She took my hand and tugged me toward the back and out the door, but stopped as we got to the alley. Tamara Gale and her husband were just getting into a gray Nissan Rogue.

^

Monday, October 31, night

And now, sitting here, I make the connection. The car down on the street belongs to Tamara Gale and her husband, and he's sitting there waiting. Checking his watch. Smoking. Talking on his phone.

But why is he here?

^

Sunday, October 30

When the Nissan pulled away, Z turned to me and said, "She just keeps getting crazier."

Z drove an old Jetta wagon. She opened the rear hatch first and checked the video gear that was packed in the back, covered with a blanket. When we got in the car, I asked her how she knew Tamara Gale.

"She's my mother."

"And you work for her?"

"Sort of. She thinks I'm her videographer. What I'm really doing is . . ." She seemed about to reveal a secret, then censored herself and said, "Well, my own project." She pulled out a small amber vial and unscrewed the top. She dipped the tip of a key from her key ring into the vial and offered me the first hit. It had a combination of flavors: a medicinal smell like rubbing alcohol combined with something earthier. The numbing at the back of my throat told me cocaine, but a moment later I knew I had just snorted a speedball, and that the heroin had a kick to it.

Z watched me as she helped herself to a small pile of the white powder for each nostril and then offered me a second one. It was going to be an interesting evening.

She drove away from the beach and then north a bit, finally turning onto a tree-lined street in the most expensive part of Santa Monica. Her battered car didn't fit the fine old houses, but she pulled into the driveway of a white Georgian home with two massive oaks in front. The driveway took us to a three-car garage topped with a guest apartment.

The ringing in my ears had settled down, and I was ensconced in a rosy glow of contentment, marveling at Z's ability to negotiate the narrow parking spot, her competence, her strangeness. Her hand landed on my thigh, and the fanged snake looked alive and ready to strike. Fingernails in black polish scratched at my jeans and Z said, "Let's go up."

We left the video gear in her car and climbed the stairs. I turned and looked back at the garage: a Range Rover and a new Jag, expensive hanging bicycles, a pair of standup paddle boards suspended from the ceiling, everything pristine and new except for the Jetta. I was so high I felt as if I could fall forward and float over it all, as if I were roaming but still in my body.

Z didn't care much for furnishing or stuff. The apartment was one large room with a kitchen at one end and a bathroom at the other. In the middle, there was a futon mat on the floor with pillows piled up at the wall end. An ashtray and Chinese takeout cartons were strewn around it, some clothes and a towel on the floor in a heap next to a dresser near the bathroom door.

There was a guitar on a stand, an old sunburst Gibson J-45 that must have been worth a fortune. Its pick guard and soundboard were scratched and worn away—somebody had a busy strumming hand.

And there were books. A head-high bookcase was packed with hardcovers: Cocteau, Sartre, and Camus packed in next to Lorca, Borges, and Fuentes. On another shelf were psychology books: Jung's *Man and His Symbols*, various books on consciousness, and William James' *Varieties of Religious Experience*. Yet another was devoted to psychic phenomena, telepathy, clairvoyance, and reincarnation. Some of them were clearly skeptical in nature; others purported to offer scientific evidence for the paranormal. I leafed through some as Z made tea. At the end of the shelf, pushed back as to be almost out of sight, was a copy of Tamara Gale's book. I pulled it out and joined Z on the futon.

The food cartons and clothes and towel had been picked up. A tray with two cups of tea, honey, and slices of lemon sat between us. Nice British biscuits with chocolate were piled on a dish adorned with Chinese dragons. Z—whom Dave had dubbed Zombie girl—was an interesting package indeed.

"There's something strange about you," she said, chewing on a biscuit and watching me as I added lemon and honey to my brew.

"I've heard that before, but never from someone who had fifty-one-fifty tattooed on her neck." The number refers to a California legal code that authorizes involuntary psychiatric confinement for people deemed to be a threat to themselves or others on the basis of a mental disorder.

"Third time was a charm. I had to commemorate it."

"What happened?"

"My psych meds didn't like my street meds. They had a war in my brain and I lost."

"No fun."

"Nope."

"So could that happen at any time?"

"I told the doctors to fuck off. So now the street meds keep me pretty even. Of course, I don't really cop on the street—the heroin is from a connoisseur's ancient horde of Persian white and the coke comes from Bolivia straight to my guy—but you know what I mean." I did know what she meant—she was plugged in, like my friend Jimmy, and had clearly been at it for a long time. She lit a joint and took a long pull on it before handing it to me.

I was never much of a recreational user. Getting high wasn't a party for me; it was, at first, surcease from chronic pain, the result of an injury. Later, using was primarily about quelling the pain of not using. My ex-wife, Allison, would be quick to point out, however, that the original injury that set the ball rolling was in fact due to my being drunk while riding my bike.

But this was new behavior for me, launching into an orbit of pure delirium, methodically advancing toward a state in which sensation was all that existed. When she stretched her impossibly long neck toward me and touched her lips to mine, a whole new set of chemicals exploded in my brain. A sense of urgency and physical power, modulated by the grounding quality of the opiate high, led us to a trance-like dance of undressing, lips locked, tongues exploring and retreating, teasing and testing, until, finally free of encumbrances, we rolled together, left, then right, then off the mat and onto the carpet, rolling and touching and licking and sucking, no hurry, all in a liquid, languid rush of animal heat.

CHAPTER 23

Dave used the flight to New Mexico as a time to organize his thoughts. He had a legal pad on the opened food tray and started to jot down bullet points that he hoped he could use to create a diagram that could help him make sense of what was going on.

He started with his first contact with Tamara Gale, writing *TG, Billy Taft, December last year*. He made a note that there had been a month-long gap between the teen's death and Tamara Gale's initial interview and subsequent information leading to the boy's body.

The next entry read: *TG, Kyle Johnson, last April, two-week delay*.

He had detailed notes on each case, but for now just wanted an outline, a skeletal structure he could flesh out later.

The third item was the one that had him flying to New Mexico: *Last week, YouTube video, predicts poisoning?* He added several question marks, as it was by no means clear that she had predicted anything.

After that he added the event at the high school he was about to visit. Was it a separate event, or part of item three? And what about the call from Peter Riddle, the man who connected the Tamara Gale prediction with the New Mexico poisonings?

Dave had run the name through several systems. There were a surprising number of Peter Riddles in the country, including one in federal prison for racketeering and another in the Leon County Jail in Tallahassee. A Google search showed an attorney in Newark, a triathlete in Portland, and a drag-queen lead singer for a Prince tribute band. There was nothing to go on with the name. Just a random lonely guy who watched bad TV shows and the news.

Fourth on Dave's list was the over-the-top, swooning performance of last night. He pictured Tamara Gale on stage, like an opera star in the final tragic movement, wailing out her vision of violence.

Next, he listed Jerry Ayres and his threat to expose Tamara Gale as a fraud. He noted that Ayres claimed to have files on each of the Gales and that he had promised to broadcast them today, adding in large print: *BAD FOR DEPARTMENT*. To have a discredited showbiz psychic associated with the PD made for bad press and credibility problems. Van Evera was pissed, and Dave sensed that he could be the sacrificial lamb in the outcome.

Then there was Theresa Brewer from Channel 7, who clearly had some sort of contact with Tamara Gale. Was there a PR person? Dave didn't think so. Tamara Gale wasn't there yet; she was still bush-league, priming her résumé and aiming for Oprah. Dave had called Brewer and got the usual bullshit about sources.

He fired up his iPad and opened an app that generated Venn diagrams. Then he created a series of circles and filled them with the contents of his new list. When he dragged them into a cluster, the overlapping circles had Tamara Gale in the center, with no other commonality that he could see besides Brewer, and that didn't help. He color coded each circle, but it didn't help. He didn't have enough information.

Chapter 24

Monday, October 31, night

So Philip Gale is watching me from his car on the street. And Tamara Gale is Z's mother. And I got high with Z, had an extended blackout, and now I am here alone.

Except for Philip Gale.

Should I go down and talk to him?

The Jack Daniels is gone. I open the Bacardi and pour a spot into a fresh cup of coffee. Once again, I take inventory of my chemical arsenal: a couple of Dilaudids, a half gram of sparkly coke, and the Naloxone—the heroin user's Plan B in case of overdose.

Actually, by the time you're high enough to need it, you're probably not going to remember to use it. Naloxone is technically known as an opioid antagonist. When administered intravenously, it quickly hijacks the receptors that heroin and other opiates bind to and reverses the effects dramatically. It can obliterate the high and the pain relieving effects for any user and can send a junkie with a habit into dire withdrawals. Police and other first responders carry it in most states, and worried parents with strung-out teens keep it on hand for the dreaded but all-too-likely event.

As I stare at it, I remember the last time—the only time—I ever used it.

∧

Monday, October 31, early morning

The sex was grand, but when the party goods faded our priorities changed. This time Z brought out a rig and measured amounts of white powder from separate vials. She fixed me up first and then found a spot on her arm. The snake tattoo did a fair job of obscuring her tracks, but soon she would be looking for new veins to hit.

Somehow I found myself lying on my side. I hadn't noticed the transition, but now I watched Z as her eyes closed, then opened showing only the whites. There's a place on the moon called the Sea of Tranquility, and I was floating on it, a minute speck of awareness in the void.

Time drifted by. We rolled around some more, in a dream of tangled limbs and detached hunger.

Finally, Z got up and went to the bathroom. She came out ten minutes later wearing a silk robe and a new demeanor. The robe was nice; the attitude, not so much.

"The fuck is your problem?" She looked down at me with a sneer. Six feet of very strange creature. There was a twitch in her cheek and her snake hand was drumming against her thigh.

"Didn't know I had one. What's up?" I could only guess that she had rebalanced her drug combo, opting for uptown in the fast lane.

"You think you can come over to my place and fuck me and then go through my shit the second I leave the room?" I looked around, wondering where "her shit" might be stashed. Kitchen cupboards, maybe? The dresser?

"Don't know what you're talking about. I haven't moved since you got up." I had, in fact, been lying in a post-coital, heroin-induced dream zone that had been extremely pleasant until just a moment ago.

"Where do you know my mother from?" Now she was demanding, threatening even, as she stood above me. She stepped over me with one foot and abruptly sat on my chest. "You work for her, don't you?" There was a strange glint of hysteria in her eyes; whatever she had injected in the bathroom must have been powerful to cut through the opiate haze. Who would even want to do that?

"Never met her in my life. My friends told me to come see her act, or presentation, or whatever she calls it."

"HER FUCKING CLOWN SHOW is what I call it!" The bones of her ass were digging into my ribs. "And who are your friends?"

Things were getting so weird, I had to make a choice: what would take this down a notch? What could make it worse? I opted for the truth.

"A cop and a journalist. The cop is the one your mother gave information to about the two boys that were found murdered. The journalist is the guy who said he was going to expose her tomorrow"—I looked at my watch—"I mean today, on his podcast. He thinks it's all bullshit and wants to bring her down."

She stared at me for a moment. It was getting hard to breathe. I was assessing my next possible move—grabbing her wrist and rolling, swapping our positions and changing the dynamic—when she finally said, "You're telling the truth, aren't you?"

"Yes, I'm telling the truth. Now get the fuck off me and try to act human."

She didn't move. She had seemed about to mellow a bit, but then tilted back toward the new crazy. I guess she didn't like something I said.

"Nobody tells me how to act." The malevolence in her eyes was not reassuring: we were escalating. When she leaned forward and pinned my wrists to the ground, I brought my legs up and crossed my ankles around her neck and then rolled forward in a snap movement. She was on her back so fast she didn't have time to blink. I got up and said, "I'm gonna call a cab."

I reached for my pants and heard a sob. Now it was my turn to look down at her. Her hair was a crazy mess, her kimono was open, and her face had twisted into a look of tearful anguish. She said, "I'm sorry. Please don't go. I'll make it up to you. I don't know what came over me. Don't go." She reached up for me, and like an idiot I took her hand.

My wife Allison turned out to be crazy. She hadn't started that way—I don't think—but sure wound up on the loony edge of the bell curve. And in college, I dated a girl who wound up in UCLA's Neuropsychiatric Unit because she was convinced that the CIA and the Mexican Mafia were after her. Maybe we attract what we are, or I have a soft spot and a caretaker problem with damaged psyches, but once they go big-eyed and helpless and sad, I'm a chump.

CHAPTER 25

Dave had an interview with the Tohatchi High School principal at one o'clock, which gave him just enough time to rent a car and get to the campus. It was a two-and-a-half-hour drive from Albuquerque, where he had landed at ten o'clock. He had to drive west past red-rock mesas and the El Malpais National Conservation Area, turning north at Gallup, on through the flatlands and the town of Ya-ta-hey, and finally arriving almost on time.

He parked and walked through a hallway toward the administrative offices. Students were rushing to class, late from their lunch break. One of the girls was wearing cat ears and had drawn whiskers on her face with a marker. It occurred to Dave that it was Halloween.

The principal, a broad-shouldered former football player named Craig Owens, got up from his desk to introduce himself. Dave had checked him out: forty-four years old, clean record except for some sealed juvenile stuff, married, two kids, played for Arizona State.

The office window behind Owens' desk looked out at a bright-green football field and, beyond that in the distance, drab-brown low hills. The sky was a severe blue with windswept clouds. Dave sat and apologized for being late.

105

"It's okay. It actually worked out, as I wanted to have Carlton Tallman of the Navajo Police come by, and he couldn't make it until"—he checked his watch—"right about now. I don't know if you've heard, but this is now officially a murder case."

"One of the kids died. That's why I'm here." One of the students in the ricin attack had previously had an asthma condition and was especially vulnerable to respiratory problems.

"Yes. Never left the hospital. Two of the others will have problems for the rest of their lives. The parents are desperate, and the students are freaked out. The community is split over whether to continue the football season." His phone buzzed and he pushed a button. A secretary announced a visitor.

Owens went to the door and ushered in a small, wiry man wearing jeans and a crisp blue work shirt. The biggest things about him were his worked-silver belt buckle and his ten-gallon hat. He stuck his hand out to Dave and said, "Carlton Tallman." He had a deep bass voice like an old FM radio late-night disc jockey, and his face was wrinkled and brown like a shopping bag that had been crunched into a ball and then partly smoothed out. His snakeskin boots had steel toes and looked brand new.

Carlton Tallman didn't seem to mind looking up at Dave. His grip was firm and his gaze friendly, alert, assessing. When they sat, he addressed Dave.

"We're deeply concerned about this event. We welcome any help or information, but I need to know why you're here."

Dave had hoped Van Evera would have prepped the locals on the nature of his visit, but clearly that hadn't happened. He explained the tie-in to his own cases, glad he had organized his thoughts on the plane ride.

When he got to the part about Tamara Gale's so-called vision of a bird and young people rolling on the ground, Tallman, who had been nodding his head and taking notes, looked up and said, "This was how long before the event?"

"Five days prior," Dave said. "And then we got a call in. After the event was on the news, some citizen called us and tied it to the televised interview in which Tamara Gale had made her alleged prediction of a disaster. He also called the news stations and the tabloids, and they ran with it, which is why the press on the event exploded."

"Yes, we thought it was a lot of coverage for a local event—even one as unusual as this was," said Owens. "It certainly fanned the flames here. A lot of people here put stock in prophecies and psychic powers."

Tallman waved a hand dismissively. "That's not quite accurate. The community has a different view of these things than the mainstream, but they're not gullible about every bit of horseshit that shows up in the *National Enquirer*." He turned to Dave and said, "Where did that call come from?"

"Some guy, local LA cell phone, said his name was Peter Riddle. I couldn't find anything interesting about him. Tried, but—"

Tallman interrupted. "You don't find it strange that someone in Los Angeles saw a news report that hadn't made it as far as Arizona? And that same guy had seen the show with the so-called psychic?"

"Well yes, of course it's odd. Maybe he knows someone from here who told him about it. I don't know. What I do know is that now Tamara Gale has predicted another disaster, and I want to know what her connection is to all these events, because she's the common denominator and it doesn't make any sense."

"We have next to nothing. We've got one student who happened to see something, but he was drunk and throwing up at the time and therefore not a reliable source. And we have no way of making a connection."

Dave was ready to follow any lead that came up. "What did he see?"

"He saw a man sitting in a car in the parking lot during the game. The man was looking at a laptop, and it looked like he was playing a computer game."

Bingo! The drone operator. "That certainly sounds like our man. Did you get a description? What kind of car? Anything?"

"Yes. The car was a gray Nissan SUV, and the man had a scar on his forehead. The kid didn't get the plates, and we've already run all the local vehicles and recent rentals. So far it doesn't go anywhere." Tallman stared out the window and his eyes tracked across the sky as if following a bird's flight.

It was an obscure connection, the kind of long shot that can lead down a rabbit hole into a maze of false leads and hopeless tail-chasing, but Dave thought he might have the missing piece to the puzzle.

Chapter 26

Z made coffee, and we each had a brief blast from her heroin/coke combo vial. It was enough, but barely. My body was remembering the inevitable timeline of heroin-high maintenance—perfect degrades to okay and then devolves to inadequate, not-at-all okay, and finally to cramping, nauseous misery. Unless you do more.

Z seemed to be back on the planet. While the coffee brewed, she had brushed her hair and put on purple lipstick, leaving the bathroom door open and chatting cheerfully as if nothing strange had happened.

Biscuits again. I suddenly realized I was famished. Food is a quirky item in the drug cycle. I wasn't really hungry, but I needed sugar badly. I loaded up the coffee with fake creamer and demolished six of the biscuits. Apprehensive about setting her off, I threw out what I hoped would be an innocuous gambit.

"You mentioned a project. What's that about?"

"Long story. You sure you wouldn't rather do something else?"

I thought about it, imagining the feel of her silk kimono, the way it would slide off her, the rolling and the wrestling and the ferocity of her climaxes. Maybe later.

The sun was coming up, and birds were chirping in the trees, but junkies don't care; they have their own cycles to pay attention to, and their inner clocks are set to the demands of their habits. I was aware of Mindy at home, wondering where I was—I had been deliberately ignoring my phone—but somehow I couldn't assign a value to that as a problem, nor was I in any shape to go face it.

"Are we in a hurry?"

"Not me." She leaned forward and kissed me, leaving my lips oddly sticky and fruit flavored.

"So your mom is a psychic." I wondered if I could learn anything that could be useful to Dave. For that matter, I wondered how Dave's evening had gone; he was pretty loose behind the juice when I left the bar.

"My mom is a sneaky bitch bullshit artist. I shoot her shows, but my project is going to fuck with her act big time."

"It sounds like Jerry Ayres already has a plan to expose her."

"Yeah, he's been hounding her for months. I should make him part of my documentary."

"So is Philip your dad?"

"That creep? Hell no. My dad died when I was little, and then Mom hooked up with Phil and boom—instant nightmare!"

"He did things?"

"No, not that kind of stuff. We all played the perfect family: Christmas photos at Macy's, Brownies and Girl Scouts. Mom did the PTA. Phil coached soccer. It was all a charade."

"How's that? You just hated the whole middle-class act, or was something wrong?"

"Wrong? It was rotten from the inside out. Here's an early memory of life with Phil: We were driving back from a summer vacation in Big Bear—we rented a cabin there every year. Mom had gone home before us in her own car. I'm in the back seat, almost asleep—I'm like seven at the time—and we're back in the flatlands at the base of the mountain. Phil stops the car and some kid gets in. He's like fifteen or sixteen, hitchhiking. We go on for a few miles and they're talking low and I see Phil checking me out in the mirror, but I've got my eyes almost closed. He says, 'Hey, Zini, how's it going?' and I pretend I'm asleep. The next thing I know I can see through the space between the seats that the kid has his head in Phil's lap and is bobbing up and down."

She shook her head at the memory and then looked up at me and said, "I mean, how fucked up is that?"

"Pretty fucked up. So what did you do?"

"I didn't know what they were doing, but I knew it was creepy. I closed my eyes and thought about how much I hated him, and Mom for marrying him. Finally, he pulled over and gave the kid some money and the kid left. Shit just got weirder and weirder, but the family facade was the main priority. 'Aren't those Gales the most charming family?' I could have puked hearing that."

"So when did she decide to be a psychic?"

"Some time while I was gone, I guess. She used to want to be a movie star. She wrote this book about her life that was mostly bullshit—that's gonna be in my film."

I told her I had seen it and mentioned the part about the lake and how it didn't fit the factual history of the area.

"Yeah, well, big surprise. But I do remember that she always liked to do magic tricks, even when I was little. She and my real dad would take turns: card tricks and coin tricks and making things disappear. I loved it. He was like a god to me. And I was his little goddess."

"So what happened to him?"

"One day I came home from school and my mom said, 'Daddy's gone and he's not coming back,' and there was Phil, standing there with his arm around her."

"Did you ever find out what happened to him?"

"No, but I think they killed him. I left home when I was fourteen. I lived on a commune for a while, out in Colorado. I got passed around enough that I decided if I was going to have sex a lot I was going to make money at it, so I moved to Denver. I got in the dope business, too. Eventually, a rich boyfriend put me through film school, at least until I dropped out."

She started preparing another rig. She raised her eyebrows at me, as if to ask if I was ready.

She had tied me off and had just slid the needle into my arm when she said, "By the way, I'd be worried if I were your friend Jerry. He definitely shouldn't have threatened my mom like that."

CHAPTER 27

Monday, October 31

Dave's cell phone chirped as he was driving up the San Diego Freeway from Los Angeles Airport.

He had used his time on the return flight to fill in the details in his Venn diagram. Each circle got its share of facts. He used his finger to swipe the screen and move the circles around so they overlapped in different ways, but the common denominator was always the same: Tamara Gale. But now there was a new component, a man with a scar. And that fit into at least two of the circles: the show last night and the man with a laptop in a sports utility vehicle in the Tohatchi High School parking lot.

Tamara Gale's husband.

It was eight at night, and the freeway was clear and moving fast. He picked up his phone on the second ring and heard Van Evera say, "Where are you?"

"Just passing Washington Boulevard, heading north on the 405. I got a lead for you, but I don't know how good it is—"

"Never mind that," Van Evera interrupted. "Weren't you with a guy named Jerry Ayres last night?"

"Yeah, we went to see Tamara Gale and then had a few drinks afterward. Why?"

"Because he's dead, is why. We've got a team there now, and you're going to join them. Finn is there." Finn was the crime scene investigator, a very smart and thorough guy that Dave had always liked.

"What have we got so far?" Dave was floored. It made perfect sense, even though it seemed so far-fetched.

"Not much. The ME says it happened last night, but no sign of forced entry. Asphyxiated—plastic bag over his head. The place was completely turned over, so somebody was looking for something."

"Who called it in?"

"The victim shared a house. Boyfriend, renter, I don't know. Has his own room; says they're old friends. He's a nurse at Cedars-Sinai. Worked a twenty-hour shift and got home earlier tonight. You'll get more when you're at the scene."

"I'm on it. Text me the address."

"That's not all."

"Okay, what else?"

"The deal you were at last night, the fucking psychic clown show?"

"Yeah, what about it?"

"Just like you predicted, it's all over the news. Tamara Gale predicting a disaster, and there's a shot of you sitting there in the audience. A fucking officer of the LAPD at a psychic fucking clown show. And Theresa Brewer identifying you."

Van Evera clicked off. Dave knew that if he had been on a desk phone it would have been slammed into the cradle.

CHAPTER **28**

Monday, October 31, daytime

This one hit me harder. Bells ringing, a sudden lurch in my heart, and a distant voice telling me to breathe. With huge concentration and effort, I took a breath; it was like lifting a weight too heavy to get more than a couple inches off the ground. I let it go.

"BREATHE!"

Okay. I lifted again. Two inches. Too heavy. Dropped it. She slapped me.

The day went by. We did it again.

And again.

Did it all.

Time floated by. Z had gone through another flip into the dark side, only this time she didn't take it out on me. She screamed into her phone and stomped around the garage apartment, kicking her guitar off its stand at one point and yelling "Fuck, fuck, fuck!" at the floor, at the ceiling, out the window.

Apparently we had run out of dope.

I tried calling Jimmy but got his voice mail. He was living with his mom, recovering from a bullet to the chest and waiting on a felony hearing, so I doubted he was good for a hookup anyway.

She settled down for a bit, and we sat listlessly, smoking a useless joint and swapping hits from a bottle of Rémy Martin. Finally, her phone rang, blaring a loop from an old Lou Reed song, and she snatched it up eagerly.

"What? Okay, whatever, fine. When?" She tapped the screen and put the phone down. "We're good." Her expression changed from the bitter, haggard one that had taken over in the last few hours to one of relief—that anticipatory high again.

I couldn't get the song out of my head: *And I guess I just don't know, Oh, and I guess I just don't know . . .*

At some point it occurred to me to ask, "What did you mean when you said Jerry shouldn't have threatened your mom?"

She was sitting across from me on the futon mat and fussing with a hangnail, chewing on her lip and trying not to vibrate. I could see the tremors start and stop as she checked them. Whoever was on his way was working on his own schedule.

"My mom is a vicious, vindictive, paranoid sociopath," she said, "and Phil's her proxy. If she even thinks you're in her way, she'll pull out all the stops to stay on top. She creates adversaries and crushes them. We had a neighbor once who had a workshop in his garage. He made stuff there that he sold online, some kind of laser-etched sign business. His wife had MS and was in a wheelchair, so he needed to be at home all the time. My mom didn't like the screech of his table saw and sent Phil to deal with it." Z's phone lit up with a text and she brightened. "Five minutes, thank fuckin' god. Anyway, the next day the table saw screeched. That night an ambulance came and took the neighbor away—somehow he had lost the fingers on his right hand. Oddly, Phil was out 'running errands' at the time. When the neighbor came back from the hospital he put the house up for sale and moved out. Never saw him again."

"So you think she would physically harm Jerry to stop him from carrying out his threat?"

"I would put absolutely nothing past her." She put her finger in her mouth and bit the hangnail off, then watched it bleed.

A car door slammed in the driveway.

The connection looked like a college kid. His name was Paul and he worked for an animal hospital. He had an expensive leather satchel that he put on the kitchen counter. Z looked at it hungrily but he didn't move to open it.

"Fuck, Paul, you know I'm good for it." Z's voice had a whiny edge. Her upper lip stuck slightly to her teeth. It wasn't pretty.

"We had this conversation on the phone and it's not changing now. Catch up with the six hundred you owe me, and you're good for a couple hundred now. But you've got to make it good by tomorrow or I'm done fucking around. Really." He put his hand on the satchel, ready to pick it up and go.

It occurred to me that I had a chunk of Ratboy's cash in my pocket. I pulled it out and counted out six hundred dollars and put them on the counter. Then I took three hundred more and held it up and said, "We good now?"

Z poured us each a shot of Remy and we moved to the fun part of the transaction. Paul had a bank bag in his satchel. The bag contained quarter-ounce chunks of shiny white flake, each in a separate Ziploc bag, and a collection of one-gram amber vials of white powder. It was the best-looking coke I had ever seen, but then coke's never really been my thing.

"I won't have any new H until tomorrow, but, like I said, I got these." He pulled out a packet of white pills. They were shaped almost like guitar picks and were scored down the middle for easy breaking. I recognized them as 8 mg Dilaudids and the bells started clanging again in my head.

His prices were ridiculous, but I didn't care. I bought a vial of coke for each of us and enough Dillys to last us until the next day. Before he left, Paul reached into the satchel and said, "Hey, gimme another hundred." I handed him another bill and he said, "Hope you don't need these, but it looks like you should have them around." He handed me two packets that had the inscription "MAD Nasal Intranasal Mucosal Atomization Device with 3 mL Syringe and Vial Adapter." Then he fished two little boxes out and said, "You should preload these. Every second counts." The writing on the boxes said, "Naloxone Hydrochloride Injection USP 1 mL, 1 Single Dose."

Paul was a twenty-first-century entrepreneur. He wanted to keep his clients alive so they could keep contributing to his cash flow.

CHAPTER 29

Monday, October 31, night

Jerry Ayres' house was on Stanhope, a few blocks south of the Santa Monica Airport. It was a million-dollar, nineteen-fifties stucco box that anywhere else in the country would have been worth a hundred grand. The street was buzzing with city cars: EMTs were still there, a couple of black-and-whites, Finn's '99 Vette, and the Medical Examiner's gray Plymouth. The ME was sitting in his car, smoking.

Two patrolmen were standing in the living room, flanking a man seated on a sofa. The man was clearly in shock, and he looked up at Dave hopefully, as if an explanation could be found that would undo the events of the last twenty-four hours and return his world to normal.

Dave nodded at the man and walked past him, following one of the patrolmen. A hallway led to three bedrooms, one to the right and two to the left. The farthest one on the left had been set up as an office. Jerry Ayres' body sprawled grotesquely in an Aeron chair, a black trash bag over his head cinched with a Velcro strap around his neck.

The room had been trashed. Empty desk drawers and their random contents littered the floor. Whoever had been searching for something—and Dave had no doubt who it was—had clearly gone from frustration to rage, as an expensive PC tower had been hurled against a wall.

To the left of the desk an old projection screen had been set up. A camcorder on a tripod had been knocked over and lay on the ground. Dave recalled Jerry's threat to expose Tamara Gale on a podcast—clearly this was his recording setup.

Dave heard a toilet flush and then water running. Finn came out of the bathroom, drying his hands on his pants. He was a big man, once a power forward at a minor college, and looked like he should be cutting down big trees or training weightlifters, but he was soft-spoken and highly perceptive.

The patrolman left the room. Dave knelt by the camera and said, "Have you checked this?"

Finn said, "Yep. The MicroSD card is missing. Don't know if that's what the place got ripped apart for, but the perp either found it or it's around somewhere."

"This kind of venting"—Dave gestured toward the hole in the wall where the desktop PC had impacted—"indicates he didn't find what he was looking for."

Finn went to the body and said, "Ready?"

Dave nodded. Finn undid the Velcro fastener, which he offered to Dave. Dave put it in an evidence bag. Finn lifted the trash bag off Ayres' head, handing it to Dave.

Dave had seen a lot of bodies, but this was a punch in the gut. Even though he had just met Ayres, they had dined and drunk together in the past two nights and his affection for the man now turned to a deep sorrow. And anger. No way did Jerry deserve this.

His nose was broken and there were burn marks on his face. His eyes were open and expressionless; he would have looked like a beat-up drunk in a stupor, except for the fact that his mouth was sealed with duct tape. The left end of the silver tape hung loosely, as if it had been ripped off and reapplied—probably by a left-handed person.

Finn said, "I wonder why he didn't just give it up, whatever the perp was looking for."

Dave knew, or at least he could guess. Jerry's fundamental integrity had an extra component: a sense of outrage when it came to deceit and violation of principles he held dear. Dave could imagine Jerry in a mounting fury matching the rage of his tormenter, helpless to override the stubbornness that would cost him his life. On reflection, Dave realized that Jerry knew he was about to be killed, regardless of his compliance, and made a conscious decision to endure whatever was coming.

He went to the front door and signaled. The ME, now standing with some officer in the driveway, walked past him, smelling of cigarette smoke. Dave was glad he had quit, but right now he could feel the pleasure of a hit off a Pall Mall and missed it: the lighting, the holding, the mouth-pleasure, the taste, the inhaling, the exhaling. He went back in to interview the roommate.

The man on the sofa looked up as Dave entered. He was in his early thirties, still wearing hospital scrubs. Over them he wore, oddly, a herringbone jacket. He was a small man, and the coat didn't fit him.

Dave introduced himself and sat next to the man. "Sorry about this, but I'll need to know what happened, from your perspective. I know you've already told your story."

The man gripped the lapels of the jacket and pulled them together. His face was still drained of color, and he shivered slightly. After a moment, he seemed to make a decision. He let his hands fall to his sides and straightened.

"My name is Brian Simmons. I don't think I mentioned this before, but Jerry's my uncle. I mean, he was, I guess. My mom's brother. I last saw him yesterday evening. He was about to go to a show, some psychic he loved to make fun of. He said he was picking up a new friend, Charlie somebody, in Venice first. I went to work—I work at Cedar-Sinai—long shift. Got there at ten last night; off at six tonight. I stopped for a beer and then went to Whole Foods and didn't get here till eight." He fidgeted with the jacket again. "Who did this? Why would someone do something like this?"

Dave stared at the man's hands. The lapels. The herringbone jacket.

"When did you put that coat on?"

"I got home and called Jerry's name, but when he didn't answer I went to his office. He works all odd hours. When I saw him like that, in the chair like that with the bag . . ." He shuddered. "I suddenly felt really cold, so I grabbed the jacket and put it on and then called 911."

"Where was the coat?"

"In the living room. That's where I went to make the call. I couldn't stand being in the room with him like that."

Dave pictured Jerry in the bar, patting the breast pocket of his herringbone jacket and saying, "I've got her whole story right here." He put his hand out toward Brian Simmons and said, "Do you mind if I take a look at the coat?"

The kid looked perplexed for a moment but then nodded and shrugged out of the coat. Dave reached into the inside breast pocket and felt a small plastic object. He pulled it out and palmed it, pretending to search the rest of the pockets before returning the jacket. "We're going to do everything we can to find out who did this, and then we're going to put him away. You with me?"

The kid nodded. Dave handed him a card and said, "We'll be in touch. Call me if anything occurs to you that might be useful." He excused himself and went out to his car, slipping the clear plastic box with the SD memory card into his pocket as he walked.

When he was out of hearing range of the other officers, he called Charlie. Still no answer, so he left a voicemail saying, "Charlie, I don't know what the fuck is wrong with you, but you've got to call me." Then he left yet another text: *PHILIP GALE DANGEROUS.*

CHAPTER 30

Monday, October 31, night

Sometime during my vigil, Daniel came to me again, I think. Call it a visitation. He came to me in his roaming body, or maybe it was a hallucination. All I know is that I was sitting at the kitchen table in a trance state somewhere between a dream and a blackout, and suddenly there he was, sitting across from me. This time, he wore shiny black And1 basketball shorts and a wifebeater. He was lithe but defined. His head was shaved and it glistened with sweat.

He said, "You don't even remember what happened to you, do you?"

I picked up on the weird alliteration of *yous* but had no idea what he was talking about. I shrugged.

"Charlie," he said, looking solid enough, though I don't recall letting him in, "you can rebuild tissue and bone any number of times, but the thread that connects you to it can only take so much abuse. And when that goes, you go."

I blinked, processing, a number of times, like a cursor on an old, slow Mac, and finally said, "Where?"

"I don't know, Charlie. That's past my pay grade."

I considered the consequences. To finally die and be done with it. Isn't that the ultimate goal, to "rest in peace"? To go on to the proverbial better place? Or at least, to black out and stay that way? I stared at Daniel, who considered me patiently, as if he expected a response. When none came, he said, "Charlie, do you want to live?"

And there it was. The question woke me up a bit—enough to reflect on my pathetic half-life, my decade of poor decisions, my chronic self-pity, my habit of evading the truth, my clear inability to be useful or available to those I loved, and my compulsion toward gradual suicide through opiates.

I looked around the bleak surroundings of Ratboy's dingy apartment. I picked at a crack in the Formica at the edge of the kitchen table. I took a deep breath, preparing to finally admit that I didn't care, that there was nothing left, that it was too hard to go on. As I wallowed in my personal darkness, a single thought germinated, took root, and then bloomed: Mindy. I saw her alone, unable to go back to her bitterly angry alcoholic mother, and abandoned by her coward of a father. A seismic event in my heart pushed a word to my lips and I said "Yes" in a pathetic sob. *Yes, I have purpose. Yes, I am willing to endure.*

"Good," Daniel said. "That's where it all begins." I suddenly recognized his voice as the voice that had guided me through the strange process of self-repair. I asked him how he could possibly know how to do that, and he launched into an explanation about all the information in the universe being in a repository, like a library, and that, with the right mode of concentration, one could access it like reading a book.

"That sounds a lot like Tamara Gale's spirit-guide bullshit."

"Perhaps. But you recovered from bullet wounds." He had me there. Then he said, "Look, we've had this conversation before. Now maybe you're ready to hear it."

"Fine. Whatever it takes."

"It's simple. You have a calling. Follow it, and you'll have a chance."

I asked him what that meant, *a calling*, and he said, "Death is a greedy motherfucker. Our calling is to intervene. And then you're responsible for the survivor."

"How will I know?"

"It will be right in front of you."

I nodded in assent, remembering my first encounter with it.

When he left, he said, "There will be trials ahead."

I don't remember if he used the door.

^

I scroll through the rest of my texts. There are too many to bother with, and a handful of voicemails. The latest one is ten minutes old, from Dave. And a text, right after, also from Dave. I check it and see: *WARNING. PHILIP GALE DANGEROUS.*

It's time to check things out. I look back at my body, once more slumped at the table, and roam down to the street.

Philip Gale is about to get out of his car. He has no idea that I have left my body and roamed down to greet him, to watch closely, to gauge his intention and methods. He has no way of knowing that I'm there with him as he checks the magazine on a silenced Ruger and slips it into a shoulder holster under his pea coat. His phone lights up and a new text from "T" says *Now!* He taps back *Going* up and gets out of the car.

I return to the body. It's sluggish for a moment, a combined result of roaming too long and accumulated toxins. I get up and open the door, leaving it slightly ajar. I go back to the kitchen table and pour a glass of the Bacardi 151 and then walk back to stand by the door. I take a cigarette lighter with me. There's no plan; I'm taking actions on autopilot, like a bird building a nest.

My mind clears and I finally remember what happened to me.

^

Monday, October 31, afternoon

Z walked Paul out to his car. I don't know why; she was dying to take a hit. She was probably trying to talk him out of an extra bit of dope for the premium price he had just charged me. A bit more stash just for herself. Classic junkie behavior.

I used the time to prep the Naloxone rigs and crush two of the Dilaudids.

When Z finally got back, we cooked and filtered the Dillys and banged them at the same time.

There's a bodysurfing spot called the Wedge in Newport Beach. During certain summer swells from the south, the Wedge produces a freakish wave that reflects off a jetty and triples in size and then dumps explosively several feet from shore. When a twenty-foot wave crashes in two feet of water, you get what's called ragdolled—thrashed and bounced off the bottom and thrashed some more. That's what happened when I pushed the plunger and injected the drug.

I didn't know that Z had put a massive dose of coke in the mix, but I knew something was wrong right away. My last thought before my heart stopped was of something Daniel had told me two months earlier, though it seemed like a lifetime ago: *If you are gravely threatened, leave the body before it gets damaged.* I left my body and watched as it went into a seizure.

Convulsions aren't pretty. I looked like a mackerel on a pier, trying to flip its way back to the water. Flecks of foam spouted from my lips and collected on my cheeks. My left hand—the side I had injected into—was inert; my right hand was quivering like a rusty banjo string. Z sat in a nodding stupor and watched me with what seemed like fascination, as if I were a pile of jelly in an earthquake.

Finally she seemed to snap into reality. "Oh, fuck, Charlie, what the fuck, Jesus, fuck . . ." as if she could chant me back to life with obscenities. I looked down at my body as the flopping subsided. It made a loud gasping sound and then stopped moving, mouth open and eyes staring up past me. Z, moving in slow motion, fumbled around for a Naloxone rig and stabbed me with it.

From my vantage point floating above and looking down at the spectacle, I knew that my body was reacting to two opposing chemical overdoses: a stimulant and a depressant. The cocaine had caused the seizure, but now the opiate had shut down my respiratory system. Or, worse, my heart had blown up. I didn't know, and was helpless to intervene. I just knew that my time separate from my body was limited, and that I might be minutes or even seconds from a permanent disconnect.

And here once again I experienced the threshold dimension—call it Purgatory, the Lobby to Hell—and I saw the drug world's newly dead: strung-out housewives and bikers, stockbrokers and students, state-prison lifers and jailhouse suicides, Skid Row drunks and tattooed white-trash tweaker punks. I saw Oxy ODs, respiratory failures, exploded hearts, HIV and Hep C victims, their tickets punched, their dance cards expired, all desperate for a second chance. Hungry ghosts longing for another shot—whether of dope or at life even they don't know, and nor do I.

And I saw the shape of Death, also hovering, waiting for me to expire, a triangular absence of light like a giant stingray, dark as an extinguished star. I had seen it before, shuddering in a feeding frenzy, blue streaks of electricity rippling through its wings as it devoured the essences of people who had meant to do me harm. Now it was here for me.

I was out of time. The dark form moved toward me as I moved toward my body. And, once again, my body received me. It was damaged, but I was beyond reach and the collector of souls or whatever it was receded, gave what seemed like an angry twitch, and disappeared.

Throughout this vision I was also aware of Z, whose drug tolerance was clearly greater than mine, talking on her phone, saying, "No, that's bullshit. No. I'm trying to sleep. Don't come over," getting more agitated as she listened to whoever was on the other end. She hung up and started going through my pockets. She used my phone and tapped the screen and spoke into it urgently. I heard her give her address and then say, "Hurry. Get him the fuck out of here."

CHAPTER 31

Dave broke protocol and put off the whole process of booking evidence and filing his preliminary report. He made a mental note of the fact that they hadn't located Ayres' cell phone, but didn't put it in the report.

He needed to get to Charlie Miner's place, but first he had to stop at home and see if there was anything useful on the memory card. It was getting late, he was sleep-deprived and overstressed, and he hadn't had a drink since his plane ride from Albuquerque. He didn't need a diagram to put Philip Gale at the Jerry Ayres murder scene or the New Mexico aerial poisoning, but how did those relate to Tamara Gale and the two boys whose bodies she had located for the police? And what was the deal with her display at the end of her performance— her "horrible vision"?

By the time Dave got home, it was past eleven. He had stopped for a bottle of Chivas Regal but then decided on Old Crow at half the price. "Make that two," he said at the counter, and he had the cap off of one before he even started his car.

He set up in the kitchen. His laptop, a four-year-old Hewlett-Packard that was so slow it could only be repaired with a hammer, had a slot for the SD card he had found in Ayres' pocket. Along with the bottle of Old Crow and a tumbler, he had a plate

130

of Triscuits and a Moosehead from the fridge. He glanced at his phone: still nothing from Charlie Miner. Dave hoped he hadn't lost two friends on the same day.

When the laptop finally booted up, he inserted the memory chip and waited. Drink, Triscuits, wait. Finally, the video program loaded and an image of Jerry appeared, standing in front of the white projection screen. He had what seemed to be a remote control unit, presumably for the camera, in one hand and Tamara Gale's book in the other.

Dave felt a twinge of regret, as if Jerry's murder were somehow his fault and could have been prevented if only Dave had been more attentive, more focused, more tuned in to the total wrongness of the Tamara Gale dog-and-pony show. He knew he deserved whatever heat Van Evera was about to rain down on him, that he had failed the department, failed Jerry, maybe failed Charlie Miner. He picked up the tumbler and took a slug of Old Crow—it didn't measure up to the Chivas, but it would do—and watched Jerry on the screen, dressed as he had been the night before.

He bobbled a bit, then righted himself and looked at the camera. He seemed a bit unfocused, blinking a few times and standing there with his mouth open for a moment before he got himself together and said, "Hello, ATOM friends. We're going to have fun with this today"—he held up his copy of *Yesterday, Today, and Tamara: My Life as a Psychic*—"just like I promised last week. And last night." He gave a horsey laugh. "I actually went to Ms. Gale's quack show and watched her pretend to commune with spirits, and guess what I found out? She was communing with her husband via a hidden earpiece! Yes, freethinkers and fellow fraudbusters, I actually walked in on her husband reading prompts from a laptop in the dressing room! And that's just the cherry on top of this poison parfait."

Dave paused the video. Ayres was clearly enjoying himself. He had an undeniable presence that Dave wouldn't have guessed at, like a seasoned comic on a roll, or a popular university lecturer, confident in his audience's approval.

The beer was good after the crackers. The Old Crow was better warm; he was glad he hadn't iced it. Some ibuprofen and he might start feeling human again. He restarted the video.

Jerry held up Tamara Gale's book. "Here," he said, "is a classic example of what ATOM exists to expose: bunk, balderdash, hogwash, hokum, hooey, and twaddle. No, let's get real"—a gleam in his eye now—"Horseshit! That's what it is. Last night's show? Forty bucks to see her hoodwink three hundred otherwise intelligent, affluent adults—that's twelve thousand dollars for an hour and a half spinning fairy tales.

"Here's what's up, friends of the real universe. Tamara Gale wants you to believe that she talks to a Persian princess from another century, that she can diagnose your health problems and fix you with magical cures, and that she has had this talent since she was a little girl. Now, what do we call this? All together now—" He gestured with his left hand as if conducting an orchestra. "Horseshit!" He giggled, a strange, goofy sound that didn't help his credibility as a champion of reason.

"I've taken the liberty to do some research, and I've found out that Tamara Gale is an invented name, as is her husband's—Philip Gale. Philip Gale got his name the way most criminals get fake names: he borrowed it from a dead person. Then he married Tamara and gave her a new last name. But wait! There's more! Gotta love the internet." He opened the book and took out a piece of paper and displayed it for the camera. "Here's a screenshot of an entry on the County Recorder's site from Vigo County, Indiana, transcribed from the original microfilm. Tammy and Peter Riddle, brother and sister, placed in foster care in 1965—the same year that Ms. Gale claims to have met her Persian princess at Lake Webb near Bakersfield, according to her book." He giggled again, and then burped. Dave realized that Jerry was still drunk and that the video had been recorded last night after the show. "And here, a year later in the Terra Haute Tribune, we have this picture of two charming young runaways." He held up a printout of a grainy old photo. A blond girl of about seven and a slightly younger boy, taller and also blond, stood in front of a small brick house, flanked by a family of five that they clearly hadn't been born into. The caption read "Missing Children" and asked people to call the police if they had any information.

Dave stopped the video again.

Peter Riddle. The name of the caller, the one who had linked Tamara Gale's hummingbird vision with the poisoning of the high school students in New Mexico.

Chapter 32

Monday, October 31, afternoon

The Naloxone took effect at the same time I merged with my body. The sensation was so horrible that I wished for a moment that I had been consumed by the Reaper, reduced to streaks of lightning in a triangular black void. My entire body felt like a root canal by Dr. Mengele. The Naloxone did its job thoroughly, flushing out the accumulated opiates that had flooded my brain during my binge with Z and replacing them at their receptor sites. It was a merciless purging of all relief from pain, physical and psychic. I wanted to scream, but only a croak came out.

I remember Z leaning over me and shouting, "You've got to get the fuck out of here. Phil's coming over. Someone saw us leave together last night. Something's wrong. Get up, godammit, get the fuck up!"

I pulled myself up to a sitting position. Phil could feed me to a wood chipper for all I cared, as long as I didn't have to feel what I was feeling. I held my hand out and Z helped me up. We went down the stairs and out a back way to an alley. Jimmy was waiting there in his silver Hummer. Z must have redialed the last number I had called, in a desperate attempt to get rid of me, and here was my old friend and heroin connection, looking at me in concern and guiding me into his car as if I were a hospice patient.

Z came to the window and said, "You're kinda fun, Charlie Miner, but you should stop messing with drugs, like entirely."

I told her thanks, that my ex-wife used to tell me the same thing.

"Okay, whatever, but you need to bail now. I don't know what's up with Mom and Phil, but they're on a rampage."

As we pulled out of the alley, an SUV raced by. A gray Nissan Rogue.

Jimmy Ortiz was a body builder and a heroin addict. I had dragged him into my last problem, and he still had a bullet wound and a court case to show for it. I first met him at my physical therapist's office, back when I was juggling three doctors in order to meet my daily Vicodin quota. One snort out of Jimmy's vial of white powder and I never looked back.

I told him I needed some help—a gun, for starters. He said he had to get back to his mother's house, that she was having her own medical emergency, and that the police had taken his guns when he got arrested.

"You keep getting into some weird shit, Charlie," he said, heading down Montana toward Lincoln Boulevard.

"It might be about to get weirder. How about this—can you take Mindy with you until things get sorted out?" I was still in massive pain, but it had resolved itself into a burning clarity. I was in trouble, and I had to keep Mindy safe.

Don't be No Evil

Chapter 33

Monday, October 31

Dave polished off the Triscuits and the beer, trying to line it all up. It made perfect sense, but it made no sense. Unless . . .

There was a key somewhere that, once turned, could unlock the whole pattern, make it decipherable and actionable, but it was elusive. Like one of those things where you say, *It's on the tip of my tongue*. He stabbed at a key on the laptop to start Jerry's video again, but missed and hit something that froze the system. In frustration, he swept the laptop off the table and watched it clatter on the kitchen floor. He had two and a half novels on it, and he wondered if he had made a mistake not backing them up.

The bottle of Old Crow was now on its side, leaking whiskey onto the table. Dave picked it up and set it right. The top was gone. He realized he had overshot the mark, and he didn't care. He knew that if he was out of booze—if he didn't have half left in this bottle and another to back it up—that he would have sopped up the liquid on the table and sucked it out of a sponge.

He went to the bathroom and relieved himself and then washed his face. He looked bloated and haggard, and his skin color alarmed him. From the medicine cabinet he took a prescription vial and shook out two Adderalls and chewed them dry.

He pocketed two more and went to his room and opened his safe. There was a Smith & Wesson M&P .40 there, a nice one with the Tritium night sights. He grabbed it and an extra clip, along with a pair of handcuffs and the unopened bottle of Old Crow.

His phone chirped in his pocket. He stabbed at the green "Answer" button, relieved to finally be hearing from Charlie.

"Philip Gale is coming up my stairs."

CHAPTER 34

Monday, October 31, midnight

It's time.

I call Dave and tell him what's happening. He says he'll be right over.

I put the phone in my pocket and step over to behind the door. The tiny apartment feels like a trap. A gust of wind threatens to open the door further but subsides. I hear him on the stairs, cheap strips of concrete in a metal frame that rings at every foot-step. He's not very interested in stealth; his heels click at every footfall on the landing. There's a hes-itation at the door. Does he sense me on the other side, thumbing the wheel on my lighter, touching the flame to the cup of Bacardi? Does he hear the whoosh of the 151 as it feeds the blaze in my hand?

It seems he doesn't. The door opens and he steps in, gun in hand.

I say, "Hey, chump," so he'll look at me. He does, and swings the gun to his right but not fast enough. I hurl the burning rum in his face. Three silenced shots go off as his finger spasms on the trigger. He drops the gun and starts flailing at his face. I step over to the kitchen and grab the Bacardi bot-tle and swing it at his forehead. It catches him on the bridge of his nose and shatters. He falls back and lands almost perfectly in the beanbag chair, stunned. The Bacardi catches fire as it flies through

138

the air and lands randomly on the floor, the walls, and the blinds on the window next to the door. Like an angry sprite, a puff of flame attacks the blowfish lamp, and it erupts in another stinking conflagration. I grab a towel from the kitchen, soak it at the sink, and then envelop the remains of the lamp with it before the heat can melt the wiring insulation and really cause a problem. The flames go out, but when the cold water touches the bare hot bulb, it explodes.

I look down at Philip Gale. He's still on fire. I can smell his hair burning and the stink of burning flesh. His nylon windbreaker decides to join the party and melts as the flame creeps down his shoulders, adding the acrid odor of burnt plastic to the air.

The fire is subsiding on its own, but I tamp out the remains with the wet towel. Patches of hair and skin slide off his scalp as I pull the towel away. His eyelashes are gone, and his slightly chubby pretty-boy look will never be the same. Blood is leaking down the side of his nose from a deep cut where his right eyebrow had been.

I close the door and drag his now- unconscious body to the kitchen and up into a chair. A quick search of Ratboy's drawers yields a lucky find: a roll of black duct tape among a variety of screwdrivers and light bulbs and junk.

I start with his hands, which I bind by the wrists to the metal struts that support the chair back. Next, I wrap a couple of feet of tape around each ankle, securing them to the legs of the chair. Then I go to the bathroom to get something of Mindy's that might be useful.

He's going to hurt when he wakes up.

CHAPTER **35**

Dave noticed an odd combination of odors as he climbed the stairs of the run-down apartment complex. He was feeling better; the Adderall had done its job and kicked him into a reasonable state of alertness, cutting through the fog of the booze. Still, he had some in the car. It was promising to be another long night.

When he knocked on the door, Charlie called out that it was open. The smell was stronger now. Whatever it was, he hoped it wouldn't attract attention. On the other hand, in this part of Venice, people didn't like to call the police.

He entered with the Smith & Wesson drawn. The air was thick with the smell of burning. It was like an old incinerator in the days when people burned all their trash in the back yard: plastic, leftover food, newspapers. Through it all he caught the unmistakable odor of rounds recently fired. He closed the door and put his gun away and stared at the jaw-dropping scene he had walked in on.

A man was duct-taped to a chair, unconscious, severely burned and bleeding. Parts of his melted windbreaker were fused to the skin on his arms, and most of the hair on his head had been burned off.

Charlie sat around the corner from the nightmare in the chair. There was an array of objects on the kitchen table, arranged with the meticulous precision of an OCD sufferer, all at right angles and equal distances: a cigarette lighter, a can of hairspray, a hand-held mirror, an empty bottle of Jack Daniels, a small amber vial with white powder in it, a hypodermic needle, some pills, and a second injection kit that Dave recognized to be a Naloxone rig. At Charlie's far right, forming the corner of a frame to the entire array, was a silenced Ruger SR22, the snout of its suppressor pointing across the table toward the unconscious man.

Philip Gale was about to do some talking.

Dave pulled the third kitchen chair out from its place nearest the door and set it across from Charlie's so they were flanking Gale.

They sat in silence for a while. Charlie, Dave noticed, wasn't looking that good: his skin was sallow, his hair was matted to his head, and he looked like he had slept in his clothes. A sad bunch, the three of them, Dave thought, but at least he and Charlie had a shot at seeing better days.

Philip Gale—or Peter Riddle, as things had turned out—might not be so lucky. Dave pictured Jerry Ayres with the trash bag over his head and a rage thrummed through him. He could easily have ended it for Gale—blunt force trauma with a tire iron would have been satisfying—but the man had information and Dave intended to get it. All of it.

At last Charlie said, "I can't figure out how he knew where I lived."

Dave leaned over and checked the man's pockets. He found a set of car keys, a wallet, and a cell phone. He put them on the table. The remaining fabric of the windbreaker hung heavily on one side, and Dave retrieved from the dangling pocket a second cell phone. His intuition told him whose it was and what he would find.

"Jerry picked you up here last night and drove you to the Tamara Gale show, right?" He double-tapped the phone screen and it woke up to a screensaver image of the solar system, the inner planets moving around the sun. He swiped it with his thumb and found Jerry's MapQuest application, with instructions on how to get to Charlie's apartment.

Charlie looked at it, not putting the pieces together. He said, "Whose phone is that?"

"Jesus, Charlie, it's Jerry's phone." Dave waited for the implication to sink in.

"Fuck. What happened?"

Dave told him about the scene at the house near the Santa Monica airport, the plastic bag, the broken nose, and the burn marks.

"Jerry had recorded his podcast. He had a setup in a back room he used as an office, with a screen and a video recorder. My guess is that he recorded it as soon as he got home that night, with the intention of putting it online the next day. Somewhere along the way, he took the memory card out of the camera and put it in his jacket pocket. Then he took the jacket off in the living room."

"So he got tortured for a memory card?"

"Seems like it, but I think Philip here enjoyed what he was doing. His real name his Peter Riddle, and he's Tamara's younger brother. Everything about them is phony."

Charlie whistled, his hand on the butt of the Ruger. "He came in with this. I guess he was here to clean up a loose end, though I can't imagine what it could be. So that's the 'riddle' that Jerry referred to at the show. That's what scared them."

Dave thought back to Tamara Gale's show. "What was it that you whispered to Jerry, just before he stood up and left? When he came back and challenged her, where had he gone?"

CHAPTER 36

Tuesday, November 1, early morning

Dave looks as bad as I feel. I could feel better right now, in a hurry; all I'd need to do is crush up half of one of the Dilaudids. But then I'd have to go through the whole process—cook it, filter it, suck it up into the syringe, tie off and find a vein, register, and finally push the plunger—in front of Dave. Or go hide in the bathroom. Somehow, no matter how tempting, it doesn't seem appropriate at the moment.

Dave asks me about the other night at the show, which requires an answer he might not be ready for. I decide to go for it.

Philip Gale stirs in his seat.

My hand instinctively grabs the gun, but he's not quite ready to wake up.

"So, um . . ." *Well, Dave, I can leave my body asleep and move around like a ghost and see shit you can't see. Right. And there are unicorns and fairies that talk to me in an ancient language. I mean, how can I accept the impossibility of my situation, let alone express it?*

Dave says, "Charlie, I've already seen you dead with bullets in your face, and then you come out of my bathroom all cleaned up like it was some kind of special-effects job. So spill it."

I tell him I can leave my body, that I call it roaming, and that I've been able to do it ever since the first time I woke up dead.

"Show me."

A little over two months ago, newly revived from my first encounter with death, I went to a little church on Crescent Heights in West Hollywood. I was in serious need of repair and barely animated. I could only see in dim shades of gray. I explained my condition to a priest named Father Tomás, and he thought I was kidding. I took off the baseball cap I wore to cover the bullet hole at my hairline, and he told me I needed medical help. I suggested he go to his office, close the door, and write something private on a piece of paper, and then come back out to the pews where I would be waiting. As he walked down the aisle toward his office, I left my body and followed. He locked his door behind him and leaned over his desk and wrote *Eli, Eli, lama sabachthani?* Then he took off his glasses and put them in a coffee cup and covered the page with a bible.

When he returned, I opened my eyes and said, "My God, my God, why hast thou forsaken me?" He blinked, his mouth hanging open. I said, "Also, you left your glasses in a coffee mug." He blessed me and called me one of God's miracles, and I left seeing a bit of color as the sun cast blues and yellows from the stained-glass windows onto the church floor.

I say to Dave, "I'm going to get up and go in the other room. You write down"—I found him a pencil and a Post-it note in the junk drawer—"a secret that nobody could know."

I go to the bedroom and lie down. I could stay like this, maybe forever. The exhaustion I feel is almost greater than the shrill grating of my nerves screaming for opiates, a drink, a handful of Xanax, anything to take the edge off. Instead, I roam back to Dave and watch him write. I hover over his shoulder and see him spell out letters on the little yellow square of paper: *I took a case.*

I have to laugh. Of course he did. I go back to my body and walk it back to the kitchen.

"Funny you should write something I already knew."

"What do you mean?"

"I watched you take it."

"The fuck . . .? What are you talking about?"

I hadn't remembered it until just a moment ago, but I had seen Dave, after he shot the man who killed me. "I was outside my body when you picked it up and took it back to your car. I saw you shoot Alan Hunter, I saw you pick me up, and I saw you grab one of the SentrySafe cases."

"Jesus, Charlie. You get weirder all the time."

"You don't know the half of it."

"Well, I guess we both know interesting things about each other."

"Don't sweat it. I took a few cases myself."

Dave chuckles and shakes his head. "So about the other night. What happened?"

"When Tamara Gale—" I stop and ask him, "What's her real name, anyway?"

"Tammy Riddle, as far as Jerry's research could reveal."

"Okay, whatever. When she was carrying on about sleep, I decided to take a look around. I wound up in the dressing room and saw Philip Gale—I'm gonna keep calling him that—wearing a headset and reading from a laptop. He had a split screen; half had data on audience members and the other half showed a view of the theatre from the stage. I went back and woke up and told Jerry to go check it out."

"So you leaned over and whispered to Jerry, and he got up and went to the dressing room?"

"Right. Why, what's up?"

"Well, if they had a stage camera pointed at the audience, they could have played it back later. Crazies like them are always paranoid, so it's something they would do. And that would connect you to Jerry's threat to expose them."

So I am a loose end. But not one he's going to get to tie up.

CHAPTER **37**

Philip Gale was beginning to stir. First a faint groan, and then a tentative flexing of his arms against the restraints. There was sudden scraping of the chair against the linoleum floor, and then he lurched back and nearly toppled over. His eyes opened, and he hissed at Charlie—hissed like a cat, spit flying, rage contorting his mangled features.

Dave watched as Charlie calmly picked up a mirror from the table and held it up for Gale and said, "Your pretty-boy days are behind you now, Phil-Peter, whoever the fuck you are."

Gale stared at the reflection of his ruined face and then lunged forward at Charlie, who swatted him on the head with the mirror. Then Charlie picked up the hairspray and flicked the lighter on in front of it. A blast of orange flame burst out from the can's nozzle, terminating inches from Gale's face.

Dave held up his hand and said, "Whoa, Charlie, take it easy, man."

"He doesn't seem to be in a very cooperative state of mind, and I'm not in the best of moods myself."

Gale, who had flinched backward as the heat grazed his face, watched warily as Charlie put the hairspray down.

Dave had done a lot of interrogations, but never like this. He knew the right thing to do was to call it in and do it by the book, but there were situations that the "book" didn't anticipate, characters and situations that didn't fit the standard model. Like Charlie and the psychos in the Mexican cave.

He rapped his knuckles on the table. Gale shifted his attention to him, and Dave could tell he was assessing his situation, looking for an angle, how to gain favor, lie, escape, or do some damage. They always did that. Handcuffed to a desk in a locked room downtown, their little rodent minds looked for an edge, some way to turn things around, a song to sing, someone to rat out, a deal to cut, whatever it took. But first, there was the defiance.

Dave decided on his gambit and said, "Guess where I just came from?"

A baleful glare; no response.

"Jerry Ayres' house. And guess what I found?"

Still no response, but the glare betrayed a hint of unease.

"I found what you were looking for, Peter Riddle. Old Jerry really did his homework on you and your sister."

Gale looked straight at him without moving, but his eyes did a strange thing, as if an electric current had just fired in his brain and only willpower was keeping the rest of him in check. Dave concentrated on Gale, but in his peripheral vision he saw Charlie crush up a pill and boil a portion of the powder in a spoon with a cigarette lighter. Gale's eyes flickered to the hypodermic needle in Charlie's hand as he drew the liquid from the spoon through a bit of paper towel.

"And before that I was in New Mexico, at the high school. And guess what?"

Gale closed his eyes. His eyelids fluttered and his body started to vibrate. Dave could only guess how much pain the man was in, but he knew that he was having a hard time keeping it together.

"One of those kids died. So that's two murders we can tie you to. Do you want to talk about them?"

Gale, whose body now shook in an escalating tremor, said, "I can't stand this anymore. You're violating my civil rights, and I need a fucking ambulance and medication RIGHT NOW!" The man was shouting, and he started bouncing the chair up and down and bellowing incoherently.

Dave saw Charlie raise the hypodermic needle.

Chapter 38

Tuesday, November 1, early morning

Something's got to give, and Dave's approach isn't cutting it. The creep is flipping out, and the last thing I want now is for someone to call the cops.

The crook of his right arm—the one nearest me—is exposed and the vein is popping out nicely from his exertion. I nod at Dave, who stands up and moves behind Gale to keep him still, and then I jab the needle into the bulging blue vein and deliver four milligrams of Dilaudid with a quick push of my thumb.

It happens pretty quickly, especially if you're new to it. Gale goes from rigidly straining against the duct tape to completely limp in about twenty seconds. His eyes roll back and show the whites and his face goes slack and his mouth hangs open as a gobbet of drool hangs off his lip.

"How's that going to help us?" Dave walks over to the window and peers out through the blinds.

"Give it a few minutes and I'll show you."

Dave turns and looks around. There's shattered glass on the carpet. He looks up at the broken bulb and the remains of the blowfish lamp and says, "Too bad about the booze." He shakes his head and seems to think about it for a moment. Then he goes to the door and says, "I'll be right back."

I hear him go down the stairs and figure I've got enough time. I prep the other half of the Dilaudid and jam it in my arm just as I hear Dave coming back up.

The half-life of Dilaudid is about a couple hours, which means that after about five hours it's effectively out of your system. This is no longer about getting high to party, to break down barriers between myself and a stranger, or to have long and dreamy sex; it's about trying to feel normal, to get right, to re-establish competency. That's why it's called a fix.

Still, there's no denying the high as the initial rush comes over me in a flood of relief. I manage to remove the hypodermic and replace it on the table as the door opens and Dave comes in. I don't know why I feel it necessary to be secretive about what I'm doing; after all, Dave just went to his car for a bottle, which he takes a hit from as soon as he's in the room with the door closed.

I look up at him, amused at this bear of a man, his fringe of hair betraying his age even as his smooth skin speaks of youthfulness. I am enveloped in a cloud of cotton, a wonderful sea of nothingness, a state of marvelous well-being that any rational person would want to experience as a permanent condition. In fact, I know the price, and that there will be a reckoning. But not right now.

CHAPTER 39

Dave wiped at a trickle of Old Crow on his chin and looked down at Charlie, who was clearly in orbit around a beneficent sun. Dave, who had seen so much damage wreaked by the so-called war on drugs, wondered why it had lasted so long, given its complete strategic and humanitarian failure. The answer, he knew, had a lot to do with the repeal of Prohibition—another failed experiment in social engineering. The enforcement apparatus that had been built to deal with illegal liquor was too powerful a machine to simply dismantle in the wake of the Twenty-first Amendment. Marijuana, cocaine, and opiates became the new bogeymen, sins of the Mexican and Black ghettos threatening to leak out and poison White America.

Dave went to the kitchen and got a pair of glasses and then took his seat next to the two blissed-out wrecks. He filled each glass with the cheap bourbon and lifted his to Charlie. "How much did you give him?"

Charlie lifted his own glass and took a sip. Dave wondered what booze did on top of heroin, or whatever Charlie had injected. "Four milligrams. Same as I got, but he's new to this—no tolerance. Doesn't matter, though. He'll be chatty pretty soon."

"What's in the vial?"

"Coke."

"Is that going to make him talk?"

"Not by itself."

"Mmmmm . . ." Gale's eyelids fluttered and then opened. "This is nice."

Charlie said, "Glad you like it, Sparky. There's more where that came from, you know. You're still ugly, though." Dave glanced over and watched as Charlie poured a measure of white crystalline powder from his coke vial and sucked it into his needle from a spoon.

Dave could feel that sweet spot approaching, where the new booze was taking the cranky edge off the Adderall and the combined effect was a perfect balance of calm alertness. *Alert calmness. Soporific stimulation. Motivated tranquility. Tranquil motivation.* He knew his mind was fucking with him, but it was amusing; he felt a laugh bubble up and erupt with a spray of spit. Something shot out of his nose and he wiped that away, too, and the thought came to him that his job was on the line, that this was the middle of a slow-motion train wreck, and that it was time to get his shit together.

Focus!

Dave slapped his shield on the table and said, "We'd like to get you the medical attention you need, but we need some answers first. If you'll help us out here, we'll see to it that you stay comfortable. Are you with me?"

Gale raised his head back and peered at Dave through eyes that were barely open. After a long silence he said, "My chest really itches. Could you untie one of my hands for me?"

Dave said, "I don't think so. But if we can make this quick, you won't have to put up with it for long."

"Where do you want to start?"

"Billy Taft."

"I loved Billy."

"Okay. Weird, but okay. How did he die?"

A strange sound came from Gale's mouth, a choking sob that he cut off by holding his breath. When he finally let the breath go, he said, "We got into an argument. He told me he was breaking it off and wouldn't see me anymore."

"So what happened?"

"I reached out to him and he pushed me. We had been drinking and we smoked a little weed. I grabbed his wrist and he fell with me. It wouldn't have happened if he wasn't stoned."

"So how did he wind up dead?"

"It was in the bathroom of my house. There's an old radiator-type heater there, and he hit his temple on it. It's almost like I pulled him into it."

"What happened then?"

"He wasn't moving, and blood was coming out of his ear. I was going to call 911, but I called Tamara first."

"And she didn't want you to call?"

"She said she'd be right over, so I just sat there with his head in my lap. When she got there he was dead, and she said that we had to figure out a plan to get rid of the body."

Dave pondered this, starting to see where it was going.

"And the plan was to take him to the desert."

"We drove him out there together. We put his body in the trunk."

"Why that particular spot?"

"I didn't know at the time, but then Tamara contacted you and I realized what she was doing."

"And what was that?"

Dave watched Gale's eyes as he looked down at the table, agitated now, and shook his head. "She used Billy to sell her goddamned book."

"Right." Now it was coming together.

"The fucking bitch!"

"You loved Billy."

"I did. And she knew it."

"Okay, Kyle Johnson. How did that go down?"

Gale looked across the table at the hypodermic next to Charlie. A leer crossed his damaged face, making him look deranged.

Charlie said, "Sure, it's got your name on it." The guy was already lusting for his next high.

Gale looked back at Dave and gave a dismissive shrug. "Just another junkie street kid."

"Fine, but what happened?"

"Tamara got good press finding the body out in the desert. Her book sales got a huge pop on Amazon and she started getting on talk shows. Her whole deal was about becoming a fucking star with her psychic bullshit."

"And . . .?"

"She had taken a picture of me in the bathroom kneeling over Billy's body. She's controlled me my whole life, but now she really had me. I was fucked." He looked away to his right, into the kitchen, and spat on the floor. "I picked up Kyle Johnson at the Santa Monica pier. It's easy."

"Then you killed him and made it look like Billy Taft's murder."

"It was Tamara's idea."

"And you dumped him in a drainpipe at the beach."

"Yeah. And I planted a business card on him from I guy I ran into at a meeting."

"What kind of meeting?"

Gale wriggled in his seat, rolling his shoulders and taking a deep breath before answering. "Incest survivors who act out and do what has been done to them."

"So the guy we arrested, Peterson—you set him up?" Dave had interviewed the man, who broke down and sobbed hysterically, denying everything, panicked about the idea of prison time. He was a handyman, he said, and lots of people had his card. The case was still pending after numerous delays, and the man was stuck in County Jail.

Gale nodded. He tried to scratch his chest with his chin and then closed his eyes and seemed to fall asleep. He woke with a start and said, "Tamara's fucking book went to number one on the Amazon charts. And she started getting TV spots."

"So she sent you to New Mexico."

"Fucking bitch."

Dave knew how perps' minds worked. They would spill, but they would always hold something back, a get-out-of-jail-free card that in their twisted minds would get them one-up on the system no matter what the evidence was against them. Dave wondered if they were there yet—the holdout, the bargaining chip—and what it would cost to get him to cough it up. Right now, of course, he had no case, no admissible evidence or confession, just a crazy story about a pair of sociopaths. He wondered how he was going to extricate himself from the situation and still make the arrests. And then there was the problem of Van Evera and the department's image. He could see the headlines now: COPS BUY FAKE PSYCHIC MURDERER'S STORY. And worse, they would infer that the police were responsible for the subsequent murders. He took a long pull on his drink and popped the big question.

"What's the next thing that's going to happen? She said it was going to be bad."

Gale came to full attention at that. His face twisted into a sly grin and he said, "That's the big question, isn't it, Detective? What's going to happen next?"

"Well, we've got all night, but you're going to be in a world of hurt pretty soon."

"Oh, I've known pain, sir. More than you can imagine. I wonder what my arrest is worth against the eighty or ninety lives that are going to be extinguished in just a few hours."

"Your sister would plan a mass murder in order to boost her reputation as a psychic?"

"This is Hollywood. Her ambition knows no bounds. But tick, tock, I can hear the clock, and it's not on your side."

"And you're okay going along with it all, carrying out her plans?"

"She calls me her very own Renfield. I have a different taste in body fluids, but I do serve my master. Or mistress, as the case may be." He winked, and Dave wanted to smack him, break his teeth with a hammer, as if evil could be obliterated in a single stroke.

Chapter 40

I've watched this creep for about as long as I can stand. It helps to be high—I can pretend I'm in a B movie on late-night TV, with Philip Gale in horror-show makeup and Dave as James Garner in *Marlowe*—but the fact is, Gale's smug little wink brings up a rage in me that even the opiates can't suppress.

Dave's had his chance. It's time.

I nod to Dave and he hesitates, looks at Gale for a moment, and nods back in assent. He gets up and stands behind Gale, reaching around for a choke hold to immobilize him.

I jab Gale with the Naloxone. I figure it will take a minute, maybe two, before he realizes just how fucked he is. His nice little opiate buzz will disappear, and the pain of his burns will come blasting back in an avalanche, a tsunami, a dinosaur-extinction crashing meteor of sensation. I remember my own experience of last night at Z's—excruciating, relentless, obliterating.

Gale strains against the choke hold, his eyes bulging. I watch as the light of recognition registers. His mouth opens in a garbled shriek that gets choked off as Dave tightens his grip, the crook of his elbow against Gale's throat. I jab him with the second rig, same spot as the Dilaudid but other arm, right up into the nice blue vein, and pump an eighth of a gram of Paul-the-college-kid's top-shelf coke into his system.

The Naloxone does its job and flushes the last remaining effects of opioids from Philip Gale's brain. His bulging eyes are pleading now, his face beet red. The coke joins the party and wakes him up even further, intensifying his experience. I hold up the vial and show him that there's more.

Dave relaxes his grip, and Gale opens his mouth—to scream, to curse, to beg?—but only a croak comes out. He starts to shiver. I worry that he'll have a stroke—an eighth of a gram is a hefty dose—but worse things could happen. He could just pass out, a bonus for him and a loser for us.

I hold up the needle. He stares at it, his mouth a small O, and then his eyes dart over to mine. I say, "I can give you another nice warm blanket like the first shot or we can keep you like this for as long as it takes, but you need to tell us about the plan—what it is, where, when, how—and you need to start now. Are you willing to do that?"

He nods in desperate, pathetic compliance. I knew he would, because I know how he feels. Except for the burns. That's a kicker, the bonus incentive. I feel like an Abu Ghraib interrogator, caught up in the righteous act of fighting evil, the small voice whispering that the act is abhorrent relegated to background noise. Bound, perhaps, to haunt me later.

Dave sits back down and hands me the bottle of Old Crow. Not my favorite, but this isn't a good time to be picky about flavor. I hit it hard and hand it back. Gale watches like a starving animal. He says, "She's going to be pissed now."

Dave says, "Why is that?"

"I'm supposed to bring her idiotic signs."

"What signs?"

"The signs that are supposed to tie her prediction to the event—remember? 'Signs of death.'"

Dave reaches across the table and picks up the Ruger. "What event?"

"There's going to be an explosion," Gale says. "It's timed to go off—" he pauses, then looks up with a crafty grin "—at one. After lunch." His voice is still raspy and he's gone pale, except that his burns are a startling red. He blinks his hairless eyelids and stares at the wall.

"Where?" Dave leans in so that his face is inches from Gale's. His lips are tight against his bared teeth, and there's a spasm in his cheek.

"The Wil—" Gale chokes on the rest of the word and has a coughing fit. Dave jerks away, but not in time to avoid a spray of saliva.

A staccato rapping on the front door freezes us all in our seats. There are three more loud knocks, and a female voice says, "Police!" I pick up the remaining drugs and paraphernalia and bolt for the kitchen, where I pocket the remaining Dilaudid and dump the rest into a carton of Mindy's milk in the fridge. Dave gets up and answers the door.

CHAPTER 41

Dave stood facing a cop, her hand on the gun at her side, the radio on her shoulder squawking something unintelligible. Her name tag said "Huerta." She was short and looked nervous. Her partner lounged on the sidewalk at the bottom of the stairs, looking up. Their squad car was double-parked and idling with the lights on.

Dave started to step outside but the cop said, "Whoa, hold it right there!" Dave stopped and said, "PD. I'm going to reach for my badge, okay?" This made her more uptight, and she said, "Don't move," and called over her shoulder to the cop downstairs.

Dave heard the stairs ring as the man came up. He knew that he had to block their line of sight to the kitchen table, which was only eight feet to their left. His mouth was suddenly very dry.

"Officer, I'm David Putnam, detective with the LAPD. How can I help you?"

The partner was a giant, six-five and clearly a gym rat, whose shoulders strained at the fabric of his patrolman's shirt. His tag said "Potter." The woman said, "Al, he says he's one of us, wants to reach for his badge."

The big man pulled his service weapon and said, "Okay, slow and easy."

Dave took his wallet from his pocket and opened it to display his shield. "What's the call here, Officer?" He tried to summon some authority, but it came out sounding lame.

"We got a disturbance complaint here: loud noises and someone sounding like they're in distress. Hey, what's that smell?"

Dave put his hand out for his wallet and said, "Kitchen-stove fire. My friend burned himself putting it out. Must be what the neighbors heard. He yelled when it happened. Knocked a pot on the floor. It's all handled. But thanks for responding, officers." His hand was still out. The giant had holstered his gun, and the female cop was about to hand him his wallet. Her radio squawked again, and she got a code that Dave knew was a domestic violence call. She gave him the wallet and was about to turn when a loud groan came from the kitchen.

The big cop said, "Move aside," and brushed past Dave into the apartment. The female cop had her gun out in a heartbeat and told Dave to turn around and put his hands behind his head.

Chapter 42

A huge cop comes charging into the room. He has his gun drawn and yells, "Turn around, hands behind your head, NOW!"

I've never been very good at compliance, so I sit back at the kitchen table and put my hands out flat. The table is cleared now, except for the Old Crow, the hairspray, and the lighter. I realize the last two might be hard to explain. Oh, and there's the gun.

The cop comes up behind me and grabs my left wrist, cuffs it, and wrenches it behind me, then pulls my right hand back and snaps them together. Dave gets herded in by a short Hispanic female cop who is saying something about backup and medical assistance into a mic on her shoulder.

The big cop looks at Gale, who has slumped forward and is playing dead, and says, "What the fuck is going on here? Sir, are you all right? Sir, can you hear me?"

Gale, severely burned, taped to the chair, doesn't respond. He's got to be so jacked by the shots I just gave him, I can't imagine how he has marshaled the willpower to remain totally inert.

Dave says, "Call my captain. This is part of an investigation. If you fuck this up, some bad shit is going to go down and you'll catch massive heat from it." The lady cop has him sit in the beanbag chair. She looks up at the remains of the blowfish lamp and shakes her head. "Looks like some bad shit has already gone down. You want to tell us what's going on?"

"You're looking at a serial murderer who just copped to a plan in motion to carry out a terrorist act."

"Why's he look like that?"

"He came in with that"—he nods toward the Ruger on the table—"and Charlie here subdued him. If you repeat what I just told you and it gets to the press, there'll be a city-wide panic. If you let me talk to my captain, we can pursue it, do some real police work, and hopefully prevent it. Are you on board with that?"

Huerta looks at Gale and then at her partner, who shakes his head. Despite their size difference, she seems to be the decision maker. She takes her time. Finally, she says to Dave, "The man goes to Harbor General. I'll call off the backup. This stays between us until you reach your captain and I get a clear picture of how to proceed." She thumbed her mic and said, "10-22. Disregard the last assignment."

The big cop gestures toward me and says, "What about him? And the gun? Jesus, the guy came in with a silencer? Who are you?" He's looking at me now, and not in the friendliest manner. If I look anything like I feel—and I'm sure I do—then I look like somebody to put in a squad car and take downtown.

Dave intercedes on my behalf. "He's key to this whole thing, and he's coming with me. There is no basis for holding him."

Huerta says, "We'll see about that," and comes around behind me and pulls my wallet. There may or may not be a warrant out for me. I was arrested and taken to the county jail downtown two months ago on possession charges. I got released in the middle of the night when some big money and a high-power attorney intervened, but I've been too out of it to check my status since then. It doesn't matter anyway, as my driver's license was stolen in Mexico and the one I carry is the one a tweaker made for me under the name Paul Cleary, whose blue Saturn is parked downstairs.

"Well, Mr. Cleary, let's hope you're not wanted in the system, right?"

I look up at Dave, who doesn't know all the details of my Mexican saga. He looks puzzled for a second but doesn't bat a lash.

A siren wails in the distance, getting closer. Cars pull up on the street below and doors open. Through the slats in the blinds to my right I can see police lights flashing and then the ambulance pull up. Huerta shrugs and says, "They came anyway. Guess I'll have to deal with it." She tells Potter to watch us and goes out the door.

Something about the violence of the encounter with Philip Gale, the subsequent interrogation, the partial revelation of his wife's monstrous plan, and the arrival of the police has neutralized my condition. My mind and body have been shocked into a state of near normalcy, and the need to continue consuming mind-altering substances is superfluous. My arms are uncomfortable, I could use a shower, but I'm okay. I wonder if Dave feels the same.

The door opens and Huerta returns, accompanied by a pair of paramedics. They take in the bizarre scene, the half-burnt blowfish lamp, the acrid air, the broiled human taped to a chair, and set to work unfolding a gurney and cutting Gale loose. He continues to play dead, and Dave says, "Cuff him and don't let him make any calls." He turns to Huerta and says, "Did you reach the captain?"

"Yeah, and he's pissed, but he says to bring both of you in and he'll meet you."

"Then your partner has to ride with Mr. Crispy here and make sure he doesn't talk to anyone."

"Are we booking him?"

"Just hold him at Harbor General. Get him treatment. Or don't. I don't care, but keep him isolated. And stay with him."

She takes the cuffs off both of us and gives Dave back his wallet and gun. I take my wallet off the kitchen table. Dave says, "I'm gonna need both your cell numbers. Huerta pulls out a notebook and writes in it. She tears off the page and hands it to him.

"What should we do with that?" She points to the Ruger.

"Bag it and sit on it. Or leave it. We can't book him yet. It's complicated. Meanwhile, I need his phone and wallet. Those are his keys."

The EMTs haul Gale outside and down the stairs, followed by the huge cop. The squad cars below start to disperse.

Huerta says, "Well, gentlemen, let's go."

CHAPTER 43

Dave felt a headache coming on, the kind that knows there's no relief coming down the pike so it just takes over. When they got to the sidewalk, Charlie said, "Over there, the Nissan, that's Gale's car."

Dave said to Huerta, "Get it hauled and have a team pick it apart."

"What are we looking for?"

"I don't know yet."

Huerta signaled to the remaining patrol car and told its driver about the Nissan. Then she nodded toward her own squad car and Dave realized that she wanted him to get in. "I'm gonna need wheels."

Huerta said, "Captain van Evera said I should bring you to him, and that's what I'm doing. Not negotiable."

Dave looked up at the sky, frustration compounding the throbbing in his head. A glimmer of orange streaked the horizon to the east, and he realized it was already morning. "Then you're my driver for the rest of the day, or whatever it takes."

Huerta said, "If that's what I gotta do," and they got in the car.

Dave glanced at Charlie, who didn't seem too happy about being in the back seat, on the wrong side of the metal screen. "Take it easy, pal. We're the good guys."

Van Evera had that knack that Dave could never figure out: he could look sharp in his Italian suits and expensive brogues at the end of a long summer day. He looked that way now, at six in the morning. Dave felt, along with his relentless migraine, shabby, and he knew Van Evera noticed every aspect of his condition.

Dave ran down the entire scenario: Jerry Ayres' house, the body, his video, the history of the Gales and their real names and relationship, and the events at Charlie's apartment. He left out the part about drugging Philip Gale.

Van Evera listened without interrupting. When it was over, he said, "You pocketed evidence at a murder scene?"

"The video, yes."

"And you questioned an injured suspect while he was restrained?"

"Yes." Dave could see where this was going, but he didn't care.

"And you instructed an officer to isolate but not book a murder suspect, correct?"

"Yep."

"And you left a silenced weapon at another potential crime scene so that there's no chain of custody?"

"That's correct, sir."

Van Evera sat back and shook his head. He looked over at Charlie. "Who the fuck are you?"

Dave said, "I already told you, he—" but Van Evera put out his palm and said, "Stop. I want to hear it from him."

"My name is Charlie Miner. I was with Dave and Jerry Ayres the night before last at the Tamara Gale performance in Santa Monica. I suspected that she had a hidden earpiece and was getting her so-called psychic readings fed to her. I told Jerry, who went to the dressing room and found her husband—"

"Who's really her brother," Dave said.

"—found her brother watching the audience on a laptop and reading personal data into a headset. We figure that, plus Jerry's challenge and the fact that he used the word *riddle*, is what got him killed."

"So why were you a target?"

"We think they watched a playback of the stage camera—the one Gale was watching on his laptop in the dressing room—and saw that Jerry got up and discovered the scam after I whispered something to him. That made me a loose end."

Dave felt a familiar electrical whine, like a malevolent current crackling in his temples. He needed clarity. He needed a drink and an Adderall and some Excedrin, but none of those were in his immediate future. He slammed his palm on his captain's desk.

"This is all bullshit. There's a fucking bomb, or something, going off in a few hours. You've got the whole story. Fire me. I don't give a fuck. But let's move on this."

Van Evera didn't blink. He just said, "What have we got, and what do you want to do?"

Dave said, "Just before the officers knocked, Gale was about to give up the location. All we got was 'Wil—' and then he shut up."

Van Evera said, "Wilshire District?"

Dave shrugged. "Maybe. Why not? We've got nothing else. I need a warrant to search their house."

"Based on what? You haven't booked him. You've got nothing on her."

"Based on whatever you can sell to your favorite judge. Like, now."

There was a vibration in Dave's pocket. He fished out the cell phone he had taken from Gale. In the madness of it all, he had entirely forgotten about it. There was a new text that read: *What's going on? Are you okay? Call me. There's work to do.*

Dave scrolled up and saw the previous texts. They were all from "T," interspersed with Gale's replies. The last exchange had started at eight the previous evening:

T: *Is he there?*

P: *Yes*

T: *Plan?*

P: *Best if he comes out*

The next exchange started an hour later.

T: *Time to go up*

P: *Bad call. Waiting*

Dave scrolled further and found a previous exchange from twenty-four hours earlier—probably coinciding with Jerry Ayres' murder.

T: *???*

P: *Done. No video. Got notebook.*

Dave said, "Okay, here it is. We need someone to search his car, now. There's going to be a notebook in it that he took from Jerry Ayres' house. Basis for a warrant."

Van Evera picked up his desk phone and hit a button. After a brief exchange, he looked up and said, "Bingo. A notebook and loose notes on stationary with Ayres' name on it."

CHAPTER 44

I'm in the back of Huerta's patrol car again. It smells of industrial-strength cleaning fluid, and I can only imagine the number of times people have puked, pissed, and bled all over the plastic cover of the seat. Dave's filling Huerta in on the situation. We're heading north on Crescent Heights, and I watch to my right as we pass the church where I had my encounter with Father Tomás. A few blocks later we turn on a side street and pull into a driveway half a block to the east.

After Dave's captain called in for the subpoena, we strategized as to how to deal with Tamara Gale. On the chance that she wouldn't be at the house, we decided to stall her. Dave sent a text back from Gale's phone saying that he couldn't talk and that his phone was dying. She texted back right away asking if he would be at 'the site' on time. On a hunch, Dave told her no and ignored her next volley of increasingly shrill messages, the last of which complained about "always having to fix your problems."

Now we approach the house and Huerta takes the driveway to the rear entrance, gun drawn. Dave knocks, waits, knocks again and yells, "Police!" He uses his gun to smash out a glass pane in the door, but a deadbolt stops the easy entry. A practiced kick at the deadbolt takes it out on the first try.

Dave walks through to the kitchen to let Huerta in. I'm standing in a decently furnished middle-class living room, a bit old-fashioned but pleasant in the morning glow coming in through the bay windows. A cat comes out from under a chair and rubs against my leg.

Dave has a warrant, but in fact we don't know what we're looking for. The living room is useless, as are the dining room and kitchen. There's a guest bedroom with a bed and an empty dresser and closet with a few men's clothes hanging in it. Dave runs a finger over the top of a dry-cleaning bag and examines the dust from it.

The guest bathroom yields nothing, except that it clearly doesn't get used much. The drawers are empty, and the cabinet has a small carton of baking soda, a can of air deodorizer, and some sunscreen.

I follow Dave to the master bedroom. He opens the closet's sliding glass door to reveal a row of women's suits hanging from a bar, shoes neatly stacked in a rack below. The dresser is immaculately filled with feminine items: jewelry, underwear, nightgowns. I try to imagine Tamara Gale in the lacy blue silk thing so neatly folded in the middle drawer, and wonder who it's for. Hopefully not her brother.

The bathroom smells of lavender-scented powder. It reminds me of my grandmother. The soap in the dish is purple and shaped like a bird. Everything is neat and precise.

"Are you seeing what I'm seeing?" Dave says.

"You mean am I not seeing what you're not seeing? Yeah."

"The brother doesn't live here."

"Right."

"Unless Huerta's in his room."

But we enter the last bedroom and see that it's been converted to an office. There are posters and framed photos covering the walls. The posters are all for events featuring Indian gurus: Paramahansa Yogananda, Sri Aurobindo, and Maharishi Mahesh

Yogi. There's a signed photo of Tony Robbins that says, "Don't let anything get in your way!" in a loopy scrawl. On another wall are photos of John Edward, Sylvie Brown, and Uri Geller, each signed with personal messages.

Huerta says, "I've been through the desk. There's nothing I can find that gives anything up." Dave goes through the desk's contents anyway.

The bookshelf has the predictable fare: Uri Geller's *Mindpower Kit*, Aleister Crowley's *Book of Thoth*, and a collection of books on astrology, with crystals and onyx cat statues and incense holders cluttering up the available space.

The cat comes in the room and brushes against my leg again, yowling and purring. I pull the Crowley book from the shelf and leaf through it. The Crowley tarot cards have always fascinated me; something about the images resonates on a deep level.

Dave says, "We'll check the garage, but so far there's nothing here and we're short on time."

I'm about to put the Crowley book back when I notice something red and black through the space where the book had been. I say, "Hey, check this out," and Dave comes over and removes a few more books. The red and black item was a box of fifty .380 cartridges. Dave opens it. Half are missing.

We pull the rest of the books out, but there's nothing more. Dave calls Van Evera and says, "Nada, but she's probably carrying. We need an APB out on her, armed and dangerous." He pauses, listening, and then says, "I don't know yet. I'll get back to you."

CHAPTER 45

Dave was frustrated. His headache was now a tack in each temple, rhythmically pounded by a ball-peen hammer, but he didn't care. He didn't care that he could smell his body odor, or that he was going to lose his job, or that IA was going to crawl up his ass over the way they had treated Gale. None of it mattered. All that mattered was finding the bomb, or whatever it was, and disabling it. This was what he was good at: dogging a problem until it gave up its secrets, collecting and sifting through facts until a picture emerged. Hunting.

But there was no scent. Not enough facts, nothing to dog.

He turned to the others. "Okay, what have we got?"

Charlie said, "If Gale was trying to say Wilshire, we're pretty much there."

The same had occurred to Dave. The Wilshire District was only a few blocks away. It included, depending on whom you asked, the Los Angeles County Museum of Art, the La Brea Tar Pits and Museum, a corridor of office buildings, Koreatown, and the Aroma Center, a high-end mall complex with shopping, restaurants, a gym, and a spa. Any of these would be a perfect location for a terrorist act, especially at lunch time.

His phone vibrated in his pocket. He checked it and saw that there was a text from Theresa Brewer. It said *Call me. Urgent.* He deleted it and saw that there was a previous one from her that he had missed. He had no interest in talking to her.

He took Gale's wallet from his pocket and flipped through it. The California driver license gave the address of the house they were in. There was an American Express card, a Bank of America Visa, and a debit card. No photos. Nothing personal. Forty-eight dollars in cash. A SuperLotto ticket. Dave knew that they could track his movements if they pulled his credit card records. His purchase history might yield something useful, but there wasn't time for another warrant.

He studied the photo on Gale's license and thought about the man's now-ruined face. As he pictured it, he recalled something Gale had said about how Billy Taft had died: *There's an old radiator-type heater there, and he hit his temple on it.*

Dave walked back to the master bathroom and then to the guest bathroom. No heater in either one. He tried to imagine the ongoing charade of brother and sister posing as husband and wife, but it made his headache worse. He went back to the office and said, "There's another house."

Huerta said, "So we're still at square one, with nothing. Can we get it out of Gale?"

"Maybe, if we could go back in time to before you showed up." Dave knew that wasn't fair. Huerta was just responding to a call, and once Gale made noise she and her partner did what they had to do.

Charlie said, "Can't we locate her by her phone?"

"I don't know that finding her is our main priority. We've got four hours to find an explosive device, clear a potentially crowded area, and try to disable the device."

"Maybe we can get her to lead us to it. She said in her text that she always had to fix his problems."

He should have thought of it before he called Van Evera. There wasn't anything else to go on. She was out there, presumably with a gun. What was Gale supposed to do "at the site"? He called the captain back.

"Need a location on a phone, ongoing." He swiped at Gale's phone and pulled up Tamara's number and read it to Van Evera.

"I was just about to call you. We've got a situation."

"Related?"

"Don't know. There's someone waving a gun around on the Metro. It's got the train stopped, and the one before it, and that's backing up all the others on the Red Line."

"So where is it?"

"Vermont and Wilshire. Right near you." It was a seven-mile straight shot down Wilshire Boulevard. Dave didn't like it; it felt like a diversion. Maybe a deliberate one, or maybe a coincidence, but not the target.

"We'll head that way, but I need that phone location as soon as possible."

"I'll get Clifford on it now." Joe Clifford was a hacker. His dad had worked for phone companies since before Ma Bell split up, and Joe had been an electronics freak growing up. Then he served in Afghanistan as a Signals Support Service Specialist until a truck he was riding in got flipped by an IED. Now he worked as independent consultant to Hollywood fixers and elite lawyers and as an off-the-books resource for the PD. Using him was quicker than going through channels, and Dave didn't care about protocol anyway. He could picture Clifford in his office at home, sitting in a wheelchair at a console that looked like a NASA project command center.

CHAPTER 46

Now we're racing toward Vermont and Wilshire, Huerta smashing the pedal and Dave yelling at her to take Sixth Street, it would be faster.

It's slippery back here, and I'm holding the strap to keep from sliding around. My mind is clear, but my body's beginning to feel it as the opiates lose their grip. For some reason, Dilaudids don't last as long as God's own white powder. I know what's coming: anxiety that ramps up exponentially until I want to jump out of my skin, muscle aches and abdominal cramping, sweating like a pig, and nausea. Maybe I'll puke here in this nice patrol car. That'll piss Huerta off.

I'll try not to.

I wonder how many junkies have sat right here, in this car, feeling like I do now. Straight people hate addicts; they think that we should just get over it, make a decision and stop, but they don't understand the subversion of our thinking process. And then there's the squawking of all the competing voices in the treatment field: It's a disease. No, it's a learning disability. No, it's a response to trauma and it won't get better until the trauma is processed. Each sincere; all shamelessly self-promoting.

I've seen the pathetic lines at the methadone clinics, the docs getting rich prescribing Suboxone, and the revolving-door spin-dry programs. And when I did my research and decided to try the ibogaine treatment, I went with a desperate but very real hope. What I got was my first taste of the separation of my mind and body.

I find it interesting that I can heal the physical damage to my brain and yet not this sickness: it's a different kind of damage. Daniel knows this, but I turned away from him. And then there's my friend Jimmy, who went to AA to try and stop. They chanted, "Keep coming back," at the end of the meeting, but when an old-timer asked if he had a drinking problem and Jimmy said, "Yeah, when I drink I shoot heroin," the old coot said, "That's not alcoholism," and walked away.

Obviously, my brain is telling me something. We're racing toward a disaster, and all I can think about is drugs. I let go of the strap and reach into my pocket to retrieve my last Dilaudid. I'm about to put it in my mouth when Huerta punches it around a corner and I fall sideways on the seat and lose the pill. It's somewhere on the floor, and I need to find it. I pull myself back up. Huerta catches my eye in the mirror.

"You okay back there?"

No, I'm not okay. I'm trying to hold it together back here, and my solution is on the floor somewhere, down on your nasty rubber mat, or maybe in the crack of the seat behind me, and now I've got to find it.

"Yeah, I'm good." Always say that.

CHAPTER 47

Gale's phone was vibrating again in Dave's pocket. Tamara had been blowing it up, calling and texting, and he had been ignoring it, but now it was time to send a message. He texted *in er at cedars. come get me.* He immediately got back *can't. leaving for site.* Dave typed *where are you?* and hit the send button. Huerta took a hard turn and Dave heard Charlie take a tumble in the back.

They were heading east on Sixth Street when the phone buzzed again. The text said *just leaving your place.*

Huerta hit a red light and smacked the steering wheel in frustration. Dave's cell rang. The display told him it was Clifford.

"Tell me you've got something."

"You're gonna love this," Clifford said. "She's three miles from you and just north of the Wilshire/Vermont station. Traffic is backing up all around the station. Situation in progress." He gave an address on Catalina near Beverly Boulevard.

"Is she moving?"

"Stationary right now. I'll keep you advised." Dave kept the connection.

The light changed, but the block ahead of them was jammed with cars.

The site. Was it the train station? Dave's instincts told him to close in on Tamara Gale.

"Turn left and go up to Beverly Boulevard and turn right."

Huerta put on her lights and siren and cut through traffic to head north. She turned them off when they found Beverly clear.

When they got to Catalina Street, Dave told Huerta to slow down. From half a block to the address Clifford had given him, Dave saw a blond woman getting into a black sedan. She backed out of the driveway and headed south.

Dave spoke into his phone: "Patch into Van Evera and tell him we need a car on her, or a chopper. Black Honda Civic—" He read off the plate number. "We're checking her last location." Then he told Huerta, "Pass her and go around the block. We don't want her to get spooked."

Van Evera came on the line. "What have you got?"

"The subject is moving south." He told him about the text exchange. "Right now we have to assume 'the site' means the train station, as she's heading straight for it. We need to track her, but I need to move on this location. We're pretty sure it's Philip Gale's residence."

"Got it. Keep me apprised. And Putnam . . ."

"Yeah?"

"Your circus, your monkey."

Dave had a few choice responses on the tip of his tongue, along the lines of *Bite me, fuckwit*, but kept them behind his teeth and simply hit the red square to terminate the conversation.

^

Peter Riddle, aka Philip Gale, didn't live as well as his sister. The house was a run-down clapboard-and-stucco relic of the 1920s. The gray paint had frayed in patches to the primer, and rusted iron bars protected the windows. They walked to the back on a cracked concrete driveway and found a rotting mattress on a patch of dry brown grass. Dave broke the glass on the kitchen door and they entered the house. A pair of tiny dogs yapped furiously and jumped at their ankles; their food dish and water bowl were on the floor, empty.

Huerta said, "What are we looking for?"

"Anything that pops. A message. Something out of place. I have no fucking idea."

He went to the back bedroom and found the master bath, a sad little cubicle with a rust-bottomed tub and a dirty sink. He found what he expected, an old-fashioned radiator-style heater. It had been painted fairly recently and stood out in its brightness. Dave ran his hand along the sharp corner at the top's end and tried to imagine the two of them—Gale and Billy—struggling in the bathroom, a middle-aged chickenhawk and his reluctant young lover.

He went back out and surveyed the living room. The furniture was vintage Deco, and there were framed Warhol reproductions on the wall, but the black leather and chrome had a dreary quality, as did the worn zebra-striped rug and the chipped glass coffee table. It looked like the living room of someone who used to care, who had an image of what his home should look like, but had long ago given up. A corner of the rug had urine stains and two piles of surprisingly large dog turds.

Charlie followed Dave back into Gale's bedroom. *He must be coming down,* Dave thought. He looked like he was suffering. *Like me.* It didn't make a lot of sense to have dragged him along: he was a civilian, dead weight, possibly a liability.

Dave turned slowly, taking everything in. Nothing jumped out at him; nothing *popped,* and he wondered if it would have been smarter to appre-hend Tamara Gale.

Together with Charlie, Dave methodically dumped the dresser drawers, checked the closet, the bedside table and its cupboard, under the bed, all yielding nothing but the bare essentials of a middle-aged loner living on a thin dime. No books, no fetish items, nothing to indicate a sociopath. Huerta joined them and shook her head.

Dave went back to the kitchen and opened the refrigerator. He noticed a tremor in his hand as he reached out to see what was behind a carton of milk. The fridge was old and had its freezer section inside and on top with a separate door. He pulled that open and saw pure gold, a bottle of Smirnoff 100 resting on the shelf, its sides coated with frost. He broke the seal and sucked greedily, oblivious to Huerta's footsteps as she entered the kitchen.

She said, "Hey, what the fuck?"

He took two more hard pulls and recapped the bottle. "Don't want to hear it. Whatever we're going into, you back me up, I back you up. That's all. Got it?"

Huerta stared up at him, clearly pissed, but said, "Got it," and walked back outside. Charlie came into the kitchen, saw the bottle in Dave's hand, and gestured for it. They stood there, pass-ing it back and forth, until Huerta shouted from the backyard, "Hey, give me a hand."

She had turned over a trash can by the garage and dumped the contents on the ground. Beer bottles, pizza cartons, soup cans, chicken bones, cardboard toilet paper rolls, rotting orange peels—nothing. Charlie bent and poked at the edges. Huerta kicked at a pizza box and slid it off the pile. There was a bit of fabric showing underneath. She poked at the garbage with her baton and fished out a shirt. It was beige, like the pants underneath it, and looked like part of a work uniform.

Huerta said, "Does this pop?"

garage with her. I alarmed I steal out a shirt. It was
beige, like the pants underneath it, and looked like
part of a work uniform.
Huerta said, "Does this pop?"

Chapter 48

The vodka helped.

Huerta has us picking through Gale's trash. I'm
sifting through greasy leftovers. She kicks at a pizza
box and it slides toward me. The lid flies open and
I see maggots in chunks of meat, cheese that has
turned brown, and ants swarming over it all. I back
away and stand up.

Huerta dangles a piece of clothing at the end of
her nightstick and says, "Does this pop?" Her attitude is obvious; there's something bad going on
between her and Dave. I don't care. I just want to go
back to the patrol car and find my medicine.

Dave reaches for the shirt. There's a Valero
employee badge on it, with a picture of Gale, but the
name on the badge is Eugene K. Pelletier. He checks
the pants; the pockets are empty.

Dave stares at the badge as if willing it to yield
a clue. He looks up at Huerta, who shrugs. Then he
swipes at his phone screen and says, "Joe, find me an
address and everything you can get on this name."
He reads from the badge and then says, "You still
got her?" After a moment he terminates the call.

"Joe's running the name. He's tracking Tamara
Gale. She's stationary, stuck in traffic on Vermont,
heading right for the station. They've got Virgil
Avenue cordoned off for response units, so we
might even beat her there."

We're about to go to the car, but I notice that the
side door to the garage is open. I move toward it and
Dave says, "Hey, we're out of time, let's go."

I ignore him and go into the darkness.

I fumble for a switch and find one on my left. There's a workbench along the length of the wall on that side. A single bare bulb casts a meager glow from the ceiling. Tools line the wall, spider webs occupy every dark corner, and the surface of the bench is covered with heavyweight poster boards. The top two are attached to wood handles. There's a glue gun and magic markers and extra handles. I turn on the fluorescent work light and the entire project is illuminated. At the end of the counter there's a white plastic worker's helmet.

Dave yells at me from outside, but I'm not paying attention. I pick up the top sign and flip it over. It has a crude death's head and the word *POISON* written below. I hold it up for Dave to see as he charges into the garage. He squints at it like there's secret writing he's trying to decipher and says, "Jesus Christ. Okay, that's got to tell us something."

I put the sign down. Like Dave, I'm impaired, and I can't make a connection. There's nothing else useful here, so we head to the car.

Huerta backs out of the driveway and stomps on the pedal again, making us fishtail down the street, rubber burning and me holding on to the strap. When we straighten out, I run my fingers behind me, trying to feel for my pill. I might be pushing it into the well under the seat, so I do it cautiously. It's useless, so I cross over to behind Huerta and squeeze down on the floor behind her and start feeling under Dave's seat.

Huerta says, "Would you get up and sit in your goddamned seat?" and takes a sharp left, which sends me headlong into the space behind Dave. I throw my hands out in front of me so my head won't hit the door, and there it is, my last little white rounded triangle of pure magic, butted up against the doorframe.

In ten minutes I'll be whole again.

For a while.

Chapter 49

They were heading down Virgil Avenue, lights and siren back on, making good time. Dave said, "Okay, why would Tamara even go to the location if it's got a timed device there?"

Huerta said, "I don't know. Why don't we stop for drinks and figure it out?"

He turned back to Charlie, who was sitting up in his seat again. "You find what you were looking for?"

Charlie said, "Yeah, I'm good now," but he didn't look so good.

"So, she says she's heading to the site. She's got to do something that Gale was supposed to do. He had a uniform and a counterfeit ID badge. And there's the signs. How does all that fit?"

Charlie said, "Think back to her prediction about the school in New Mexico. She said she saw a hummingbird. Then he used a miniature drone. So they plan an event and then she scripts a prediction that's close, but not too close. She has a vision of a disaster and an approximate version of it takes place soon after."

Dave processed this. Huerta pulled up to a cluster of black-and-whites, unmarked police vehicles, two fire trucks, and four ambulances. Sirens wailed at various pitches as they approached. Dave closed his eyes and pictured Tamara Gale's prediction of the next disaster. Huerta said, "Jesus Christ, are you kidding me?" but he ignored her and concentrated on the vision of Tamara's face, her expression a mask of exaggerated pain and sadness, like an opera singer's.

Huerta snapped at him. "Putnam!"

He told her to shut up and played out the rest of Tamara's histrionics.

. . . a horrible vision . . . I see . . . signs of death.

And there it was. *Signs of death.*

Dave turned in his seat and said to Charlie, "Signs of death. That's what she said before she collapsed at her show."

"That's what the placards are for! The death's heads—signs of death. She needs to be there to stage the event so it matches her prophecy. Her brother was supposed to do it, but now it's on her."

The police staging area took up most of the plaza that led to the rail station's entrance. Dave looked at the unmarked cars and recognized some of the city's top officials gathered there. At the perimeter, uniforms held the press at bay, and beyond that civilians were gridlocked in their cars.

Van Evera stood with the brass, pointing at Dave as he approached. The others looked his way. Dave recognized two captains and the deputy chief, Morales, who had graduated from the academy the year before he did but climbed the ranks relentlessly.

Van Evera said, "We've got three civilians down, one dead. So is this your emergency? Or is it all bullshit?"

"All I know is that she's headed this way." He told them about the death's head signs, the staged prophecy, and the similarity to the strategy Tamara Gale and her brother had used to create and exploit the New Mexico high school tragedy. When Morales kept staring at him, Dave said, "And when we were interviewing the husband, he was about to give up the location of the planned event."

"So what did he say?" Morales asked.

"He started to say—" Dave hesitated, knowing how lame it sounded "—a name or a location, but then he started coughing and that's when officers Huerta and Potter showed up."

"For Christ's sake, Putnam, what did he say?" Morales demanded.

"He said, 'The Wil—,' and then we realized that her residence was near the Wilshire District, so we started considering targets. Then we got the report that there was an incident here at the train station."

Morales said, "And who's 'we'?"

Dave gestured toward Charlie, who was standing out of earshot with Huerta. "That's Charlie Miner. He's a PI I've worked with before, and he has intimate knowledge about the perps in this case."

Morales looked at Charlie and then back at Dave. He said, "You guys look like you've been on a camping trip and remembered the booze but forgot to take soap."

Dave said, "Sir, I should go down there and assess the situation."

Morales said, "I think you're drunk. I can smell it on your breath. So I don't give a shit what you think. Plus, we've got SWAT and the Bomb Squad down there already, so what do you suppose you're good for?"

Dave blinked and fought back his first three responses, which included a fist, a shove, and a *Fuck you*. Instead, he just said, "Sorry, sir. I was off duty when this whole thing started."

Van Evera said, "I'll deal with you later, Putnam. Why don't you go sleep it off?"

Dave said, "Sir—" but Van Evera cut him off.

"Dismissed. And take your hophead pal with you."

Dismissed? It was ten-thirty in the morning, there was a credible warning of a bomb incident at one, and he was dismissed?

He turned and saw that Charlie was still waiting but Huerta was gone. He walked back to Charlie and said, "My boss is choking on his underwear. They get tighter when he's around big brass."

"So where does that leave us?"

"I don't know. Watch and see if it's a true cluster-fuck or a dud. Where's Huerta?"

"She went into the station. Said she was going down to the platform, see what was going on."

Dave looked over at the bosses, still huddled in their conclave. They were probably talking about the Lakers, or their next poker game. He called Huerta, but it rang four times and went to voicemail.

Charlie said, "You ever use the train?"

Dave said no. He had lived in Los Angeles all his life and had used the public transport system once, when he was a kid. The bus ride from Santa Monica beach back to his parents' house in Riverside was enough to convince him that a thumb out at the freeway entrance was a better way to go.

"Cell service sucks down there."

Dave tried Huerta again and got the same result.

CHAPTER 50

It's good to feel human again.

On the other hand, I'm keenly aware of what's ahead for me. I can either chase this till it puts me back in jail or kills me or I wind up downtown pushing a shopping cart with snot in my beard, or I can figure out a way to get free. Neither one looks pretty.

But right now I'm good.

Dave turns from his exchange with a gaggle of men in suits. He doesn't look happy. When I tell him Huerta's gone, he tries to call her. I give him a heads-up on the cell service underground and he tries her again.

A news helicopter is circling overhead. One of Dave's bosses is pointing at it and shouting. We walk back to Huerta's patrol car. Over the noise of the helicopter, Dave shouts at me, "This is all wrong."

"What part of it?" I get the feeling we've been locked out of the action. Maybe if Dave had access to a drink he could mellow out like I have.

"The whole—" He stops and pulls his phone out of his pocket. "Hold on."

He listens, pacing in circles, and then says, "You're fucking kidding me." He paces some more and says, "Unfuckingbelievable!" Then he says, "Keep on it. We'll get down there."

The chopper's lower now. Dave turns to me and shouts, "Tamara Gale isn't coming here. She detoured around traffic and got on the 110 going south."

I yell, "Where's she going?"

"The name on the badge—Pelletier—was a safety inspector at the Valero refinery."

"No shit. That's in Wilmington."

"Fucking Wilmington. Right."

"What do you mean, 'was'?"

"Joe Clifford got someone to send a squad car to Pelletier's house in Torrance. They found him and his wife dead in their bedroom."

"Silenced .22?"

"Probably. You know what could happen if a charge goes off next to a refinery propane tank?"

Valero's Wilmington refinery is a twenty-acre patch of industrial wasteland next to the Port of Long Beach. When you fly into Los Angeles International Airport, the facility is an eyesore from two miles overhead, and it's even uglier from the ground. It produces gasoline for cars, jet fuel, diesel, propane, and asphalt. Over four hundred people work there, and it's connected by pipelines to marine terminals for transport. Its safety record is decent—better than neighboring Tesoro's, or Exxon Mobil's, both of which have had explosions and fires that spewed toxic gasses for days. Environmentalists and local residents have been lobbying for years for more stringent controls.

"How are we going to get down there?"

"I've got to find Huerta." Dave takes off for the station entrance. Van Evera yells at him to stop, but he keeps moving. I go after him.

The plaza extends right to the turnstiles that give access to the Metro Red Line. I follow Dave as he vaults a turnstile and heads for the escalator. The thing moves like ice melting, but it's empty so we fly down it using the handrail to vault three steps at a time. A cop at the bottom holds out his palm, but Dave flashes a badge and says, "Have you seen

Patrolwoman Huerta? Short, short dark hair, came down in the last ten minutes?"

The cop points to the platform, where an empty train sits with its doors open. "All the action's right there." Past the stationary train, SWAT personnel are fanned out, guns pointing in the direction of the tunnel. Huerta's standing behind an abandoned kiosk, her back to us, her Glock also pointing at the tunnel. Dave yells at her, and it echoes in the huge vaulted chamber of the station. Two SWAT members spin and point their rifles, first at the ceiling, then at us. Dave waves his badge again.

Huerta holsters her gun and approaches us. "I don't think this is part of your gig. Just some whack job with an AR-15 and a lot of clips. He's yelling about immigrants. I think he's going for suicide-by-cop."

Dave says, "We need to get to Wilmington, like now."

"Does Van Evera know?"

"Fuck Van Evera. People are going to die."

"What's in Wilmington?"

"Valero refinery."

"These people are going to blow up a refinery?"

"For publicity."

"That's really sick."

"No shit."

We're heading back toward the escalator. A sudden clattering of automatic gunfire erupts from the tunnel, followed by a barrage of return fire from the SWAT team. Halfway up the escalator, my legs are killing me.

The courtyard at the entrance is clear now; the commwand staff have retreated to their cars. They know that SWAT will handle the shooter. We run to Huerta's car and tear out onto Wilshire Boulevard, siren on and lights flashing.

CHAPTER 51

Huerta got them to the 110 southbound, flying up the ramp so fast that Dave thought they might go airborne at the top of the rise.

He had no idea what they could do once they got to the refinery. Philip Gale was in the hospital, probably handcuffed to a bed and sedated. Tamara Gale was somewhere ahead of them, presumably on her way to fulfilling her destiny as a seeress, a prophet of doom, and a national celebrity. Brother and sister posing as husband and wife, playing a long game to fame and killing people to build a mythology—the pathology was too much to bear.

Dave's phone vibrated again—incoming call. He did a double-take at the name on his screen: Tamara Gale. He held up his hand for silence.

"Dave Putnam here." He tapped the speakerphone icon.

"Detective Putnam. I've had a new vision, with greater clarity, and if we hurry we can save lives together." Same voice, composed, matter-of-fact, and confident.

"Where are you?"

"I'm on my way to the hospital to see my husband. He's had some sort of accident." Now there's a curveball, Dave thought. He had texted her from Philip Gale's phone that Gale was at Cedars-Sinai Med Center, which was on Beverly not far west of their homes. In fact, Gale was at Harbor General, which was ahead of them and on the way to Wilmington. Could she be going there? Philip Gale didn't have his phone. Dave did. Could Gale have reached Tamara somehow? But then she would know they were on to her.

Tamara interrupted his thoughts by saying, "But never mind that. My spirit guide showed me how to stop this tragedy, and you are part of the plan."

"What plan is that?" He had to give her as much line as she needed, before he could reel her in. He wondered how far ahead of them she was.

"Signs of death—remember that?"

"From your prediction, yeah. And the news ran with it." Theresa Brewer had had a heyday with the phrase, repeating it six times in one report.

"They're real signs, like protesters or a march or something. I couldn't really tell. But I saw tall metal structures, and smoke, and a big V on a round white thing, like a tank. And then I saw it explode. I think it's a terrorist attack." *She's almost giving it to us*, Dave thought. But she was holding something back. Why?

"What do you want me to do with this information?"

"Find the place and get the people out of harm's way. I have to go now." The line went silent.

His phone rang again. The screen told him it was Theresa Brewer.

"What?" Dave wasn't in the mood.

"I've been trying to reach you. Tamara Gale called me earlier and gave me some bullshit about how you and I are part of a puzzle."

"Where are you?" It was his favorite question of the day.

"I'm at the Valero plant in Wilmington, covering a protest."

"How did you know about the protest?"

"Um, someone from the organizing committee called me yesterday."

"Did the caller give a name?"

"He must have—it might be in my notes. It was a man."

Probably Philip Gale. Dave told Brewer he was on his way and keyed off the phone.

He said over his shoulder to Charlie, "Tamara Gale is an evil bitch, but she's not trying to kill people."

Huerta said, "So what's the plan?" They were doing ninety and swerving through light traffic as they crossed the San Diego Freeway.

"Wing and a prayer," Dave said. "We'll see when we get there."

Charlie, who had been silent since they left the Metro station, said, "It's eleven. We've got two hours. She's the planner, he's the doer. She probably doesn't know where the device is."

Dave had been thinking the same thing. They needed Philip Gale.

Harbor-UCLA Medical Center is in Torrance, about fifteen minutes from the Valero plant. It serves as the primary trauma center for all of the South Bay area, and paramedics from surrounding fire departments are on 24-hour rotation responding to shootings, stabbings, and all manner of assaults, as well as vehicular accidents, suicide attempts, drug overdose, poisoning, drownings, major injuries by falling, by fire, or sharp object, and all the misfortunes that the average citizen hopes to avoid forever. The EMT personnel see it all, all day, every day. Dave was friends with a few of them, drank with some, and knew their stories.

He swiped his phone on and called Al Potter, who picked up on the first ring.

"You still sitting on Gale?"

"Yeah, they've got him on happy juice. He's quiet as a mouse."

"We need him."

"What do you mean? Where? What for?"

"We went to his house and found a Valero refinery worker's uniform. The badge had his picture in it, and the guy whose name was on it is dead. Gale planted an explosive device at the Valero location, and only he knows where it is."

"How am I supposed to get a sedated patient out of here?"

Dave hadn't really thought this through, but had an idea. "Stay with him. I'm going to put something together."

He scrolled through his contacts list until he found the name he was looking for. Randy Larsen was an EMT out of the Manhattan Beach Fire Department. He was a stand-up guy, liked to unwind after a twenty-hour shift, and played a decent hand of Texas Holdem. He also shared Dave's disdain for rules, bureaucracy, and incompetent command. He too answered on the first ring.

"Dave, what's up?"

"Improv time. Need a favor."

Two years ago, Larsen was transporting a gangbanger who was in a stolen car with three homies when one of them shot two members of a rival gang in a driveby. When a patrol car happened to come down the street toward them, the shooter opened fire and killed a cop. The other cop returned fire as the bangers fled the scene. One of them got a .45 bullet in the hip and went down, screaming in pain.

When Dave got to the scene, Larsen was loading the victim into an ambulance, ready to take him to Harbor General. Larsen had known the cop who got killed, so when Dave suggested a detour on the way to the hospital, Larsen and his partner were on board. A shot of adrenaline in a McDonald's parking lot yielded a name and address for the shooter.

Improv.

Dave explained the refinery situation, the deadline, and that Gale was the only one who knew where the charge was planted. "I need him at the Valero site as soon as possible. I've got a patrolman guarding him now—he can run interference for you. Can you load him up and bring him to me?"

From the back of the car, Charlie said, "Tell him to bring a dose of Naloxone."

Dave relayed that to Larsen, who told him it was standard to carry it and he would have it on hand. Dave hung up and rang Potter.

CHAPTER 52

I'm feeling pretty good, really. Eight milligrams of Dilaudid makes for a nice, punchy high. It doesn't have the kick that shooting gives, but it's definitely got legs. Too bad I had to waste some on Gale. But my time is coming; I know that, and I'm willing to endure it and see if I can get to the other side.

We cross the Dominguez Channel and turn toward the refinery. The landscape is bleaker than a crater on Mars, a rusted junkyard of towers and tanks that would make Chernobyl look good.

We pull into the parking lot by the Valero plant office building. Dave says, "Jesus, what a fucking mess."

There are three private buses and about forty cars parked together at the north end of the lot, and around three hundred people are standing and listening to a man with a megaphone. There's one news truck, and Dave says, "That's Channel 7. What's going on, and why are they the only ones here?"

Huerta parks and we follow Dave to the news crew. He says to the cameraman, "What is this?"

The cameraman points to a woman emerging from the crowd. I recognize her as Theresa Brewer, who Dave said always has the lead on the Tamara Gale stories. Now she's rushing up to us.

She looks worried as she says, "Dave, I don't know what to make of this, but I think Tamara Gale is here, handing out signs to protesters."

"Death's head signs?"

"Yes, how did you know?"

"Long story. Where is she?"

"Up near the guy with the megaphone. She's got a Dodger cap on, and a red wig and sunglasses. Jeans and a sweatshirt. She had four of the signs."

"What's going on here?"

"These are neighborhood people protesting the emissions from the refinery. They hooked up with an environmental group, who bussed in a bunch of college students and supporters."

Dave starts walking toward the crowd; Huerta and I follow. Brewer yells out, "Dave, I'm sorry!" Dave dismissively waves his hand in the air without turning around.

People are holding up signs that say, "STOP MAKING OUR CHILDREN SICK" and "SUPPORT EMISSION CONTROLS." Further into the crowd I see the first of Tamara Gale's signs, with its skull and the single word "POISON." The person holding it is a middle-aged white man in corduroy pants and jacket. His clothes and his neatly trimmed gray beard scream college professor. I ask him where he got the sign and he shrugs. "Some woman was handing them out. She had two left and went that way." He pointed toward the speaker.

Dave turns back to Huerta and says, "You need to find the plant manager and alert him to the very high probability of an explosive device somewhere in this facility, probably near enough to harm this crowd. Call dispatch and get all responders, maximum priority. Then stand by for Potter and the EMTs bringing Gale."

Huerta bulls her way through the protesters and past the speaker, who is standing in front of the plant's main administrative building. As the crowd parts for her, I see a blue cap over a red ponytail.

Its owner is handing a sign with a skull on it to an older Hispanic woman. She looks up and sees me, then sees Dave behind me and fades into the crowd, which closes back up around her.

CHAPTER 53

Charlie was waving his hand in the air and pointing to one of the death's head signs. Dave caught up with him and said, "Did you see her?"

"And she saw me. She bolted."

The speaker was blaring on about nitrogen oxide and particulate matter, sulfur dioxide and the Clean Air Act. He wrapped it up by yelling, "Clean it up!" The crowd echoed it back, first haphazardly and then with gusto until it became an energetic chant. Fists and signs—including Tamara Gale's—bounced up and down in time to each repetition. "Clean it up! Clean it up! Clean it up!"

Dave shoved his way to the front of the crowd, followed by Charlie. When they got to the speaker they stopped and surveyed the gathering, but there was no sign of Tamara Gale. As the chanting got louder, Dave saw Huerta and a man in a plastic helmet come out of the office building and approach the speaker. Huerta spoke to the man, who shook his head vehemently and shouted something back. Huerta grabbed his bullhorn and tried to warn the protesters to disperse, but they just yelled back profanities.

Suddenly an alarm went off, a whooping siren that went up in pitch and volume until it hit a crescendo and then repeated. The crowd's chanting and profanities devolved into a mixed-up jumble, lost steam, and finally dissipated as people began to head toward the parked buses.

Dave scanned the now panicking herd but couldn't see Tamara Gale. He ran back to the news van and asked the cameraman where Theresa Brewer was. The man said, "She took off with some woman about twenty seconds ago. The woman had a gun."

"Where did they go?"

The cameraman pointed toward a long, narrow, rectangular building between two giant domes on the opposite side of the parking lot. Dave motioned to Charlie, and they headed through the retreating protesters toward the building.

Charlie yelled over the siren, "You know those are propane tanks, right?"

"Yeah, and they're closest to the admin building and to the site of the protest, so they're the most likely targets."

They got to one of the tanks and walked around it, looking for anything suspicious, but there wasn't time to examine all the supporting struts, ladders, or ground underneath. There were five more of them, and that was just in the immediate vicinity. Larger tanks loomed behind this group, obscured by scaffolding.

Dave drew his .40 and approached the long, low building. Two employees came running out. One flew by, but the other stopped and said, "Are you a cop?"

Dave said, "Yeah. What's going on in there?"

The man looked Indian, or perhaps Pakistani, and wore a uniform and badge like the one they had found in Gale's garbage. He also wore a large curled mustache and a turban. "There's a woman in there with a gun. And another one—I think I've seen her on television."

"What do you do here?"

"I'm an engineer."

"If you wanted to blow one of these up, what would it take?"

The man's eyebrows rose, and he pondered the question as the siren continued to blare.

"A timed device, magnetic, plastic explosive. The whole thing could be the size of a deck of cards. I guess I would paint it white for camouflage. Is that what's going on here?" He looked anxiously toward the nearest dome.

"We have good reason to think so. You should move out to the street, as far away as you can get."

The man started running. He turned and said, "When?"

Dave checked his watch. It was eleven forty. "One o'clock."

"If we have an hour, let me get a team to search for devices. How sure are you about the time?"

Dave thought about it and realized that this whole circus was based on Gale's version of events to come, drugged, burnt, and tied to a chair.

"Not sure at all."

The man headed for the administrative building.

Chapter 54

Dave is talking to a Sikh who just exited the building Tamara Gale ran toward. On either side of the building there is a thirty-foot-high dome with a staircase spiraling to the top and pipelines running beneath them. Beyond is a cluster of domes, and past that a pod of long, white cylinders. There's no sign of the two women, so I assume they're in the building.

I move quietly into the entrance, hoping I don't wind up facing Tamara Gale's gun. The building is like a long, doublewide trailer with a narrow hallway down the middle. There's an open door to my left, and beyond it a shabby, ten-foot-square office with a metal desk and two chairs. I walk to the end of the passageway, passing seven more offices—three on my left, four on my right, all with closed doors except for the last one on the left. I look in and see a thin black man and a large white woman, each sitting on the floor and holding a bleeding wound. The woman has been gut shot and looks stupefied with pain. The man looks up at me helplessly, his hand clutching his neck. I put my finger to my lips and back out.

The exit door at the end is bolted shut. Tamara Gale and the newswoman are behind one of the six closed doors.

I walk back and Dave enters. Again, I put my hand to my lips to indicate silence. She probably can't hear our footsteps over the siren, but there's no sense alerting her that we're here. I motion toward the open cubicle and Dave follows me in.

I say to Dave, "There are seven more of these rooms. Two victims, alive but injured, in the last room to the left. Far exit is deadbolted—can't get out. She told us she was going to the hospital, and she didn't know we were already heading this way, so must have panicked when she saw us here already. She's got Brewer and she's got a gun. Any ideas?"

"We can seal the entrance and wait for backup, or we can charge every door."

"I've got a better one." I sit on the floor and lean against the wall under a window. "I'm going to go have a look."

I leave the body. As I move away from it, I watch Dave stare and slightly shake his head. I move into the hallway and then into the opposite room. The closed door is no more of an obstruction than the open one. The room is identical to the first one, except for a vase of fresh flowers on the desk. Their brilliance is in stark contrast to the bleakness of the room, the plant, the entire city.

The next room is empty—not even a chair—except for a bucket and a mop leaning against the wall. The third room on that side has a desk and an open laptop. Someone has been watching YouTube. I presume it was the Sikh, as the text looks like Punjabi.

When I move into the next room, Tamara Gale looks up sharply and moves her head around like a predatory bird, left, then right, then up as if she knows something's happening but she doesn't know what it is. She senses me, I'm sure of it, and swings her gun around the room. She's standing behind Theresa Brewer, who is seated in a cheap metal folding chair, staring at the door as if salvation or disaster might blast through at any moment.

There's a man in a plant uniform dead on the floor with a hole in his face. The room has a workbench along the outside wall, with a computer tower and four monitors. Each monitor has four quadrants, and each quadrant shows a different view of the facility. I see police cars and ambulances in the main parking lot in one of them, and the turbaned man running back toward the tanks with three other people.

I return to my body and look up at Dave. "Last one on the right. She's standing, Brewer's sitting. Both facing the door."

"Got any ideas?"

I do, but it's a longshot.

A few months ago, Ratboy—the man who kidnapped my daughter—was hiding in a cave in the mountains near Ensenada. When I shot him, his dim-witted giant accomplice charged at me. He smashed my head against the rock wall and then threw me across the cave. I left my body and watched the brute pound on it. Ratboy's body was slumped against the side of the cave, his gun still in his hand. I did the unthinkable: I entered his corpse and found that I could animate it, at least enough to raise and fire the gun. There was a price attached—I was left with the unmistakable stain of his sickness, like the stench of a swamp on my being.

Now I wonder if I can guide Dave's hand. Can I merge with a body that still has a person in it? Could I roam back to where Tamara Gale is standing and override her command on her body?

I tell Dave, "When we get outside the last door on the right, face the door and aim at shoulder height."

"You want me to shoot blind into the room? What if I hit Brewer?"

"Brewer's sitting down. I'm going to try something, but I need your permission."

"What's that?"

"I'm going to roam into the room, get the best coordinates I can, and then come out and try to merge with you so we can fire through the door."

"Merge with me?"

"It's a longshot."

"Jesus! Okay, let's go."

We approach the door. The siren is still wailing. Other sirens are screaming in the background. Dave points his gun at the door. I sit with my back to the wall again, roam, and enter the room. Gale has her phone out and is about to make a call. I line up the shot and go back to the hallway and try to move into Dave's body, but I'm repulsed as if by an elastic wall, a force field that I can feel from six inches and is impenetrable at three. It's like trying to push two powerful magnets together. I go back to the room, imagine the spot on the door where the bullet has to pass, and return to my body. I stand and ask Dave for the gun.

CHAPTER 55

Dave watched as Charlie took aim at the door. His grip was good—it looked as if he knew what he was doing.

The feeling Dave had just experienced was unlike any he had ever known. Something had tried to move in on him. He knew it was Charlie, but his mind—or something deeper than that, his *being*—treated it like a hostile invader and repulsed it. It had left him with his heart pounding, short of breath and slightly dizzy, but there was too much at stake to worry about it now.

Charlie had the .40 aimed at a spot about fifty-four inches from the floor and slightly left of the center of the door. That would be heart-to-shoulder height for a woman of Tamara Gale's size, and mere inches above Theresa Brewer's head if she was still sitting. Dave hoped Charlie had his coordinates right.

Charlie fired. He adjusted for the recoil and fired again, and then again.

Dave kicked at the door handle and the jamb splintered and gave way.

Theresa Brewer was sitting, facing the door, her mouth open, a look of shock on her face. Behind her, Tamara Gale held her hand to a wound in her chest. Blood was seeping through her fingers. Her gun had fallen to the floor. Dave realized Charlie had deliberately aimed to his left, for her gun hand and in order not to kill her. He was impressed.

He kicked Tamara's gun away from her and then helped Theresa Brewer into a standing position. He nudged the chair over to a filing cabinet and motioned for Tamara to sit. When she complied, he opened a drawer and cuffed her to the nearest glide rod.

Charlie caught Dave's attention and nodded toward one of the monitors. A paramedic was pushing a wheelchair across the parking lot, followed by two cops. The occupant of the wheelchair looked peculiar on the grainy black-and-white screen, oddly white and slumped in the chair. Dave saw Brewer's cameraman point in their direction.

The siren stopped, and a loudspeaker blared, "Emergency, Code 5, all personnel to evacuate premises immediately. Repeat: Emergency, Code 5, all personnel to evacuate premises immediately." And then, finally, it was silent enough to think. It was eight minutes before noon. They had an hour to find and disable whatever device Gale had planted.

Tamara Gale looked at her watch and said, "There are four devices, set to go off simultaneously in six minutes, that will destroy acres of this plant, and we're in the middle of them. What in God's name do you hope to settle here?"

Dave turned to her in shock and said, "Six minutes?" He had a sudden vision of Gale in Charlie's kitchen, his hesitation and sly smile before giving up the time of detonation.

"Noon," she said. "They're timed for noon. Now would you kindly get us out of here?"

A sound in the hallway caught her attention. A wheelchair burst into the room. The man in it looked heavily sedated and was covered in gauze—hands, face, and upper body swathed in it. Tamara Gale said, "Oh my God, Peter. What have they done to you?" Then she turned to Dave and said, "He has an override code. Wake him up, dammit. Or get us the hell out of here."

Dave nodded to Larsen, who pulled out a Naloxone kit and jammed the needle into Gale's shoulder. Huerta came in the room, followed by Potter, who backed out when he saw how crowded it was.

They waited. Four minutes to go.

Gale's eyes opened and he looked around, jerkily, taking in the room, his sister, Dave and Charlie, Huerta, and the body on the floor. He opened his mouth and screamed.

Dave lifted him out of the wheelchair and told Larsen and Potter to get Brewer and the people in the next room to safety. He told them they had three minutes, good luck. Potter might make a run for it, but Larsen would follow his training and his better nature and deal with the victims.

Standing now, Gale looked at Dave and said hoarsely, "I can't believe you did it again!" His lips were covered with petroleum jelly and stuck together at the corners when he spoke. Huerta drew her gun and leveled it at his chest.

Tamara Gale shouted at him, "Shut up and tell the man the override code!" She looked up at Dave. "I made him use a safety code. In case we needed to change the plan."

Gale's glistening mouth twisted into a sneer. "The code? You want the code? Okay. Got your phone? Or how about mine?"

Dave pulled out Gale's phone. Tamara looked at it and said, "That was you all this time? You bastard."

Dave thought, *Yeah, I'm the bastard*, and swiped Gale's phone on.

"Okay, creep, what is it?"

Gale looked up at the ceiling, swaying his head left and right, making a show of trying to remember.

Wasting time.

Fucking with them.

It was one minute before noon.

Finally he said, "Okay, the code. Three . . . one . . . oh . . . three . . . eight . . . two . . . five . . . nine . . . six . . . eight."

Dave punched in the numbers, knowing there was a chance that the code would trigger the bombs.

Huerta was so tense her face was sweating and her gun, still pointed at Gale, was vibrating.

They waited.

Dave looked at Charlie and said, "Is that it?"

Charlie was looking at the floor, concentrating. He said, "Let's get the fuck out of here," and bolted for the door.

Gale let out a high-pitched giggle and said to Tamara, "There is no code, you crazy bitch. Time to meet your Persian princess." He hurled himself toward Huerta. Huerta's gun went off twice before he collapsed against her and knocked her down. Dave picked her up and pushed her out the door. As they ran down the corridor, he could hear Tamara Gale yelling, "No, no, you can't just leave me here!"

CHAPTER 56

Tamara Gale is cuffed to the filing cabinet, screaming as Dave, Huerta, and I run down the hallway. I have a vision of her chewing through her wrist like the proverbial trapped wolf. My watch says we have twenty seconds. Up ahead, I see Larsen pushing the big woman in the wheelchair. Potter is carrying the thin black man on his back. They've made it to the parking lot. Theresa Brewer is standing by her news van, bent over with her hands on her knees. Dave sees them and flails his arms, screaming, "Move! Move!"

Huerta reaches the edge of the lot. It's a brisk November day, not a cloud in the sky. My legs feel like jelly. I'm operating on pure panic. The adrenaline has pushed the fading opiate high from my system and left me raw. I see Huerta sprint across the lot. I see Brewer retreat to the other side of the news van. I sense Dave behind me. I see the concrete parking block on the ground ahead of me, but then it's too late and it catches my foot.

As I sprawl to the asphalt, I hear a sound unlike any I have ever heard before, a roar of flaming madness that obliterates my world. A wave of heat smashes over me at the same time as Dave's body slams down onto my back. Another blast, and then another. The roar continues unabated and fiery objects rain down and clatter to the ground around us.

Dave's body is ominously still; he's heavy on my back, and it's hard to breathe. Ten feet away, a chunk of twisted, red-hot metal the size of a small car hits the asphalt like a meteorite. Not a twitch from Dave. The roaring has stopped, and in its absence there's no sound at all except for a high-pitched ringing, a keening pair of badly harmonized notes at the top of my hearing. I separate from my body and roam away from it.

The entire area that we just came from has been obliterated. The long, low building we left Tamara Gale in is a burning pile of charred lumber, flattened and emitting greasy black smoke that's rising to meet the billowing cloud of smoke coming from the pits where the tanks once were. Darkness at noon.

And now the shapes appear, harvesters of souls, like giant stingrays descending from the sky, menacing and predatory. They hurtle downward in a feeding frenzy: Tamara and her twisted brother, the victim in the security monitor room, the brave Sikh and his companions, and whatever other poor souls failed to evade the catastrophe are being collected, devoured, perhaps preserved, perhaps demolished, and my friend may be a target.

I look down at Dave's body, still motionless over my own. I see his pale, translucent twin separate slightly and begin to rise, as if I were seeing double, but I know the truth of the matter. I turn and see one of the shapes approach, gliding, hovering, a quivering absence of light. As it moves toward Dave's body I place myself in its path and it halts, eight feet above me, the tips of its wings rippling and twitching angrily. It moves closer and threatens to blot out the hellish sky behind it, offering instead its own hell—of extinction or purgatory or worse, I don't know.

There's motion behind me. I turn slightly, keeping the shape in view, and see Larsen and his EMT partner run up and crouch by Dave. They roll him off my body and give him chest compressions and stab him with an injection. I'm relieved to see Dave's ghostly form reintegrate with his body, and I turn and gaze at the shape above me. It radiates malevolence like a Chernobyl reactor and swoops around me menacingly, but I know that for now I am still exempt, and I see that I have earned my exemption.

Chapter 57

It's the day after Christmas, and Mindy and I are eating fish tacos on the beach in Hanalei, looking out at the pier and the surfers, delirious in the perfect winter swell. A few miles away, at the very end of the road, there's a protected lagoon for peaceful snorkeling, which we've done every day for the last week. Beyond that is the beginning of the Kalalau Trail, which will take us deep into the lush jungle above Kauai's gorgeous Na Pali Coast.

I had promised Mindy this trip before this last episode of madness, after hunting down her abductors and bringing her back from Mexico. How was I to know that Dave would drag me into another round of insanity and a new ensemble of murderers and victims, of police and media whores, of would-be heroes and authentic lifesavers?

Jimmy came through with the gold. We had to pay a premium to make it look like real income, but even after taxes it's a nice amount—enough to rebuild my house and keep us afloat and bring us to this island. And a trust fund for Mindy. I even gave some cash to my ex-wife, but now she's sniffing around for more. Most of the funds are still tied up in an investment; ironically, it's another gold mine, this time in Alaska.

Jimmy found a recovery group that he likes and just took a ninety-day chip. He says they're a goofy bunch and he hates the God crap, but it's better than being strung out. I'm glad for him. He got probation for his case and recovered from the bullet he took.

I met again with Daniel. He's the only one who really understands my situation, and I realize that I need him as a mentor in order to handle the weirdness of my redemption. He confirmed what I had already intuited, that my reprieve from death is contingent on my stepping up and participating in a meaningful way in the lives of those around me. He congratulated me on my intervention on Dave's behalf, and then said there was more work to do.

Dave spent two weeks in intensive care. Along with my warding off the predatory nightmare shape, his friend Randy's quick attention saved him from dying on the spot, but his recovery was precarious for the first week. He had been hit by the blast and then, as he was falling on me, pierced in the shoulder by a flying shard of metal. The first thing he asked me when I visited him in the hospital was this: "How did you know to run?" I told him how Allison and I, before things went bad, used to play Scrabble every morning at breakfast. That when I see words on the side of a bus, I rearrange the letters to see what else they might spell. He said, "So?"

"So the numbers he gave you—he was just wasting our time—were three . . . one . . . oh . . .—that's Los Angeles, just to keep us engaged—and the rest were three . . . eight . . . two . . . five . . . nine . . . six . . . eight." I showed him the keypad screen on my phone and watched him, waiting to see if he would get it.

He made a sour face and handed me back my phone. "It spells FUCK YOU. What a fuckin' idiot."

I had lunch with him the day before we left for Kauai, and after his third beer he said to me, "Charlie, you've really fucked with me as a writer."

He seemed only half serious, but I wondered what he meant so I asked him.

"Being around you makes my stories seem mundane. But the truth is so far out, so far-fetched, that my agent would run me out of town if I tried to use it in a book."

I thought about it. An ambitious wannabe psychic makes predictions, then sends her brother out as her proxy to make them come true. There's got to be a story there, stripped of my supernatural baggage. I said, "Just tell the stories you want to tell. You don't need the money."

He looked at me and laughed. He had thrown his gold into the deal with Jimmy, and he had his disability and retirement pay. "You're right. Maybe my Mexican dream can come true."

Z didn't make it. I talked to her after the refinery disaster. We met at The Pygmy Up, which is still my favorite coffee shop. She didn't seem too fazed by the fact that her mother and step-father were serial murderers, or that they had triggered the worst refinery disaster in southern California history. But when I told her that the man she had known as Philip Gale, her mother's husband, was, in fact, Peter Riddle, her mother's brother, she freaked out. She said, "Oh my God, that's just so disgusting," and she walked out. I later found out she overdosed and died that night, and I picture the black shape that came for her, voraciously inhaling her essence, and I am stunned by the tragedy of addiction and the wrongness of a system that has declared war not only on perpetrators but also on their victims, while blood spills like wine on a tablecloth, spreading until it stains the nation.

The End

Acknowledgments

I would like to thank the fine—and established—writers who took the time to read an unknown and then offered their kind words, especially Tim Hallinan, James Frey, Grant Jerkins, Joe Clifford, and Dan Fante. And, of course, law-enforcement veteran Dave Putnam, a friend and prodigious storyteller, for allowing me to use his name and persona in my book. And no, I have never seen him drunk.

About the Author

Daniel Earl Javorsky was born in Berlin and immigrated to the US. He has been, among other things, a delivery boy, musician, product rep in the chemical entertainment industry, university music teacher, software salesman, copy editor, proofreader, and author of two previous novels, *Down Solo* and *Trust Me*.

He is the black sheep of a family of high artistic achievers.

He can be found at www.earljavorsky.com.